ALMOST ALL THE WAY HOME FROM THE STARS

Science Fiction Short Stories

Jay Lake and Ruth Nestvold

Red Dragon Books

Copyright for the collection © 2013 by Joseph E. Lake Jr. & Ruth Nestvold.

All rights reserved. No part of this publication may be reproduced, distributed or transmitted in any form or by any means, including photocopying, recording, or other electronic or mechanical methods, without the prior written permission of the publisher, except in the case of brief quotations embodied in critical reviews and certain other noncommercial uses permitted by copyright law.

Publisher's Note: This is a work of fiction. Names, characters, places, and incidents are a product of the author's imagination. Locales and public names are sometimes used for atmospheric purposes.

Book Layout ©2014 BookDesignTemplates.com and Ruth Nestvold

Cover Design by Britta Mack and Ruth Nestvold
Cover images by isoga and Alex Mit, licensed through Shutterstock

Almost All the Way Home From the Stars / Ruth Nestvold & Jay Lake -- 2nd edition ISBN 978-1514811641

TABLE OF CONTENTS

The Big Ice 1

The Rivers of Eden 46

Visiting Bad Town 79

Return to Nowhere 83

The Canadian Who Came Almost All
the Way Home From the Stars 134

Credits

"The Big Ice" - *Jim Baen's Universe*, Dec. 2006; reprinted in Gardner Dozois's *Year's Best Science Fiction* for 2006.

"The Canadian Who Came Almost All the Way Home From the Stars" - *Scifiction*, Sept. 29, 2005, reprinted in Gardner Dozois's *Year's Best Science Fiction* for 2005.

"Return to Nowhere" - *Jigsaw Nation*, Edward J. McFadden III and E. Sedia, eds., 2006.

"Rivers of Eden" - *Futurismic*, July 2005.

"Visiting Bad Town" - *Ion Trails*, August 3005 (2005).

In memory of Jay Lake
1964 -2014

The Big Ice

"Governor-General's dead."

I glanced up from the disassembled comm-comp I'd been trying to Frankenstein together. The G-G was Core. Unkillable. But Mox didn't look like he was kidding.

"How?"

Mox's expression was more intense than during orgasm. "Field Control says the west face of the Capitol Massif collapsed in a quake. Took most of the palace with it."

A few million tons of rock and masonry trumped even invulnerable immortality. "Shit. Yeah, that might wipe out Core. Wonder what Mad Dog Bay looks like now."

"Scary stuff, Vega."

I rubbed my forehead. "Field got any instructions?"

"Hold position, maintain current activity, refuse all orders not from direct chain of command."

Think, dammit. What was important? Besides the possibility of a House coup, that is — with my brother in the thick of the plotting, no doubt. Murder most foul, if it were true.

"Why should anyone care what we do?" I asked myself as much as Mox.

For the love of inertia, we were *planetologists.* What *we* cared about was Hutchinson's World, and most of all, the mystery of the Big Ice. The unusual degree of variation in density and gravity readings. Its challenging thermal characteristics. The stray biologicals deep down where they shouldn't be.

Mostly those freaky biologicals, truth be told.

We were neither armed nor dangerous. Our station had a tranq gun, for large, warm-blooded emergencies, but there wasn't much we could do out here on the ass end of nowhere about a succession crisis back in Hainan Landing. There wasn't anything interesting about us — except me.

Mox gave me a look I couldn't interpret. "You tell me."

※

Core ruled.

It was the way of things, had been for centuries. Core

was jealous of their history, told one set of lies to schoolkids, another to those who thought they needed to know more. I'd never believed that they were the result of progressive genengineering in the twenty-first century. Smart money in biology circles was split — very quietly split over home brew in the lab on Saturday night — between a benevolent alien invasion and something ancient and military gone terribly wrong.

Some would say terribly right.

Core didn't rule badly.

They took what they wanted, what they needed, but on planets like our own lovely little Hutchinson's World, Core was spread so thin as not to matter. Economy, law, society, it all lurched on in an ordinary way for ordinary people. I had a job, one that I mostly liked, that kept me out of trouble. So far, Core hadn't done so badly by the human race, driving us to 378 colony worlds the last time I saw a number.

Core believed in nothing if not survival. I wondered how someone had managed to drop a palace and half a mountain on the Governor-General without his noticing the plot in progress.

"You still finding those protein traces in the deep samples?" Mox asked. He was back to biology, using one of our assay stations, distracting himself from disaster with local genetics. My instrument package on the number one probe was down in the Big Ice around the four-hundred-meter layer, digesting its way through Hutchinson's specialized climatological history.

I didn't need to look at the readouts. "Yup." It was slightly distressing. There shouldn't be genetic material hanging around in detectable quantities that far below the surface. The cold-foxes and white-bugs and everything else that lived on the Big Ice lived *on* the Big Ice.

It was also distressing not knowing what was happening back in Hainan Landing — but not as much to me as it obviously was to Mox. He kept glancing at the comm station, his features tense. Mox and I lived and worked in a shack high up on Mount Spivey, almost two thousand meters above the Big Ice's cloud tops.

Far enough away from politics, I had thought.

He gave me a long stare. "Anything else I need to know?"

I looked away. "Nope."

The Big Ice was a bowl, a remnant impact crater from a planetoid strike so vast that it was difficult to understand how Hutchinson's crust had held together under the collision. Which arguably it hadn't — the Crazydance Range, more or less antipodal to the Big Ice, was one of the most chaotic crustal formations on any human-habitable world, with peaks over twenty thousand meters above the datum plane.

The bowl of the Big Ice was over a thousand kilometers across, thousands of meters deep, and filled with ice — by some estimates over ten million cubic kilometers. A significant percentage of the planet's freshwater supply was locked up here. The Big Ice had its own weather, a perpetual rotating blizzard driven by warm air flowing over the southern arc of the encircling range that rose to form the ragged rim of the bowl. The storm rarely managed to spill back out, capping an ecosystem sufficiently extreme by the standards of the rest of the planet to keep a bevy of theorists busy trying to figure out who or what had ridden in on top of the original strike to seed the variant life-forms.

From our vantage point, it was like looking down on the frozen eye of a god.

Our instruments were in a cluster of military-grade shacks just above the high point of the ice-tides, deep inside that storm. We made the trip down there as rarely as possible, of course, though making *that* trip is something every adventure junkie ought to do once in their life. That long, cold, frightening journey into the depths was the main reason why we were on the Ice instead of lurking in some remote telemetry lab back in Hainan Landing. Every now and then, someone had to climb down and kick the equipment.

And deep beneath the surface of the Big Ice, below that cap of raging storm, was genetic material that had no business being there.

※

I started awake to find my sometime-lover staring at me. "Planck on a half shell, Mox! You scared the shit out of me." I stifled a yawn, my mouth still filled with sleep.

His expression was the attempt at unreadable I had begun to fear. "Field Control called back in."

"Looking for us, or just delivering another bulletin?"

"Us. Asked for someone named Alicia Hokusai McMurty Vega, cadet of the House of Powys. Took me a minute to figure they meant you."

I gazed at him a moment, rubbing my short-cropped hair and trying to wake up the rest of the way. Had I just been dreaming that he'd figured out who I was?

It didn't matter now. My cover was shot, no matter who had dredged up my full name. "What did they want?"

"Seems your presence is desired in Hainan Landing." He leaned forward. "Are you going to tell me who you are, *Vega*?"

I wasn't sure if I could. The identity he wanted from me now was one I had rejected long ago.

Maybe I could save this friendship. "When did we first meet?"

"Over six years ago," Mox replied promptly. He'd been thinking about it.

My gut turned over with something that felt like regret. "And we've been out here more than five months alone, right? I'm still Vega Hokusai, just like I've been all these years. Still a planetologist."

He locked his hands behind his back — I had the impression that he was making an effort not to touch me. Which had its own novelty; our relationship had never been characterized by impulsive, passionate embraces.

"And a cadet of the House of Powys," he pressed out.

I should have known I couldn't escape it. "We all come from somewhere. It's not who I am now."

"It's who they're asking for, back in the capital."

"Screw them." I was surprised to find I meant it.

And screw my brother, too. This would be his doing.

※

A cadet of House Powys. To graduate, to leave House training, someone had to die. A real death, irrevocable, not the strange half-life they could and did place us in for decades on end. One cadet had to kill another. Secretly. Plots shifted and revolved for years.

That was how House cadets discussed things. One death at a time.

※

When next Mox approached me with That Look, I was deep in protein analysis. Hutchinson's native gene structure was pretty well understood, though we still couldn't reverse-engineer an organism just by scanning like we could with terrestrial genes. Didn't have centuries of experience and databases, for one. It was still a small miracle how stable the underlying gene model was across planetary ecosystems: kept the panspermists going.

Either way, I didn't know what I had yet, but it was interesting — no matches in our planetary databases. Not even close.

"Vega?" His voice was low and tense.

"Uh-huh?"

"Can't we talk about this House stuff?"

I flipped off the virteo-visualizer and turned to face him. "Not much to say."

He looked up from the tranq gun he was polishing. Which didn't need the maintenance. "What are you doing out here?"

I wanted to laugh. "Mox, it's the *Big Ice.* I'm studying it, same as you. You think I'm out here plotting revolution? Against what? The cold-foxes?"

He shifted on his feet and stopped polishing the gun.

"Got another call. I'm supposed to arrest you."

Ah, Core asserting itself against whatever House effort my brother Henri was running in light of the G-G's death. Or Henri calling me in through channels, over clear?

Either way, it didn't look good for me.

I couldn't take Mox's hand now — he felt betrayed, and he would think it calculating. Which maybe it was.

I shook my head. "I may have been raised by wolves, but I really am a planetologist. Six years you've known me, you've seen enough damn papers and reports from me. Am I faking this?" I taped the virteo-visualizer.

"No . . . you're good at archaeogenetics, and you've got a decent handle on climate as well."

"And anyway, when would I have had time to run a revolution? Against *Core,* for the love of Inertia."

"I don't know, Vega."

He really was considering it. Perhaps our relationship had been more convenience than anything else, but still . . . this was *Mox.* I hadn't killed anyone since I left House, but my training — my programming — wouldn't allow me to let him do me in either.

I swallowed. "Mox, put down the gun."

He set the tranq pistol on the workbench, and I let out a breath I hadn't known I'd been holding.

I favored him with a smile accompanied by a high dose of pheromones. If I'd had a choice, I wouldn't have resorted to the manipulation, but autonomous survival routines were kicking in. "Thanks."

There was no answering smile on his face. "Now tell me why they want you in Hainan Landing."

"I truly don't know. But I'm not going back, if I have any say in the matter." I'd made my peace with Core, thought I'd seen the last of my House progenitors. I wanted no more of Henri and Powys House, no more of Core and plots and power. The Big Ice and the mysteries of Hutchinson's were my life now.

What if they threw a revolution and nobody came?

Mox glanced at the tranq pistol. "You're House. Doesn't that mean you're like another version of Core?"

I shrugged. "We're not immortal, if that's what you mean. You've known me six years. Noticed the gray hairs?"

His gaze shifted from the pistol back to my eyes. "A superwoman." It was almost a whisper.

Unfortunately, he was very nearly right, but I didn't want to go there. "Seen me fly lately?" I asked dryly.

Then number one's telemetry alarms started going off. We both spun to workstations, bringing up virteo-visualizers to an array of instrumentation.

Something was eating the number one probe. Four hundred meters below the Big Ice.

A text window popped up in my virt environment as I tried to make sense of the bizarre thermal imaging. So low-tech.

Coming for you. Be ready. Henri.

Situation alarms flared on the station monitor at the deep edge of the virteo.

Core made enemies. They controlled all interstellar travel, most of the planetary economies, the heavy weapons, and they couldn't be killed. Usually.

But for the revolutionary on a busy schedule, even cliffs can be defeated in time, by wind and rain, by frost, by tree roots, by high explosives.

The Houses were rain on the cliff face that was Core. Long-term projects established by very patient people, well hidden — some on the fringes of society, some within the busiest bourses in human space.

Certain Houses, Powys for one, raised their children in crèches as seeds to be planted, investments in the future. I was one seed, left to grow in comfort as a planetologist. My brother Henri was another, raised as a revolutionary, just to see what would happen to him.

Seeds are expendable. Houses are built to last.

※

Whatever was savaging our number one Big Ice probe, all we could tell about it was that it wasn't biological. Thinking about that gave me a bad case of the fantods.

Satellite warfare was going on overhead, judging from the dropouts in the comm grid and exoatmospheric energy pinging our detectors. Planetary Survey, ever thrifty, had put neutrino and boson arrays on top of our shack for correlative data collection in this conveniently remote location — and those arrays were shrieking bloody murder.

I figured I had an hour tops before Henri got here, with a

couple House boys or girls in case I got fussy. Henri was a Political. I was . . . something else. Something Henri needed?

What was a good House soldier to do?

I turned to Mox. "I'm going down to the Big Ice and try to rescue our probe."

He froze. "Four hundred meters deep? Planck's ghost, Vega, you can't get that far under the ice! Even if you did, you'd never make it back."

I didn't know what to say, so I didn't say anything.

We were only sometime-lovers, but still I could see the exact moment he realized. "You don't intend to come back."

I shook my head. "My cover's blown. I may as well try to rescue the probe on my way out."

Mox looked away, no longer willing to meet my eyes. "So what can I expect?"

"House for sure. Probably Core, too, following after."

"Shit."

"Play stupid. Don't mention Powys House, don't say anything about anything. Tell them I went down on a repair mission."

"And if they come after you?"

The decision made, I was already up and pulling gear out of the locker. "The Big Ice is dangerous. They have to fly through that frozen hurricane, handle the surface conditions, and find my happy ass. Accidents happen."

"Vega..."

I looked up. Mox had that intense look again, the one I had only seen in bed up till now, but he wiped it off his face before I could get up the courage to respond. House gave its seeds all kinds of powers, but bonus emotional strength wasn't one of them.

"Yeah?" I finally choked out.

"Good luck."

"You, too, Mox."

"I hope you make it."

"Thanks. So do I."

Moments later, I was outside. Day's last golden glare faded behind the western peaks. Colored lights glowed in the sky, orbital combat (coming for me?) mirrored by hundred-kilometer-wide spirals of lightning in the permanent storm of the Big Ice, glowering dark gray fifteen hundred meters below. I could smell ionization even up on Mount Spivey.

Thirty-five hundred meters above the datum plane, the air gets thin, and the weather can be pretty shitty by any standards other than those of the Big Ice.

It was glorious.

Our base shack was on a wide ledge, maybe sixty meters deep and four hundred long. Nothing grew on the bare cliff except lichens and us. Power cells and some other low-access equipment had been sunk in holes driven into the rock, but otherwise the little camp spread across the ledge like an old junkyard, anchored against wind and weather. I glanced at the landing pad, but there was nothing I could do about anyone who might arrive and threaten Mox.

On the other side of the landing pad was the headworks of the tramway running down to our equipment shacks Iceside. It was a skeletal cage on a series of cables, quite a ride on the descent. Unfortunately, the ascent required hours of painful winching, unless you wanted to climb the ladder that had been hacked and bolted into place by the original convict work crew.

I didn't have time for the tram today. I snapped out the buckyfiber wings I'd brought with me months ago and stashed against a day such as this.

Big, black, far less delicate than they looked, they could have been taken from a bat the size of a horse. There were neurochannels in my scapulae that coupled to the control blocks in the wings, wired through diamond-reinforced bone sockets meant to accept the mounting pintles. Once I fitted them on, they would be part of my body.

My gear safely stowed in a harness across my chest and waist, I opened my fatigues to bare the skin of my back. The wings, tugging at the wind already, slid on like an welcome pair of extra hands. The cold wind on my skin was a tonic, a welcome shock, electricity for batteries I'd long neglected.

I stared down into the vast hole that was the Big Ice, the crackling lightning of the storm beckoning me. I spread my wings and leapt from the icy ledge into the open spaces of the air.

One theory about the Big Ice was that it was an artificial construct. The thermal characteristics required to drive such a vast and active sea of ice had proven extremely difficult to model. Planetary energy and thermal budgets are notoriously challenging to characterize accurately, one of the greatest problem sets in computational philosophy, but the Big Ice set new standards.

So fine, said the fringe. Maybe it was a directed impact all those megayears ago. Maybe something's still down there, some giant thermal reactor from a Type II or Type III civilization come out of the galactic core on an errand that ended up badly here on Hutchinson's World.

Yeah, and cold-foxes might pick up paintbrushes and render the *Mona Lisa*.

But there were those nagging questions . . . all a person really had to do was stand on the rim wall somewhere and look down. Then they would understand that the universe has impenetrable secrets.

※

Flight is the ultimate high. The wind slid across my skin with lover's hands, and the muscles in my chest stretched as my back pulled taut. I could see the crosscurrents, the play of gravity and lift and pressure combining in the endless sea of air to make the sky road. A hurricane bound solid and slow in crackling ice, but no less deadly, or frightening, than its cloud-borne cousins over the open sea.

Below me, the lidless, frosty eye of the world beckoned.

I spilled air, leaning into a broad, circling descent that gave me a good view of the blizzard's topography. Even by the light of the early evening, the core of the storm was foggy, a cataract in the eye, but the winds there would be very low. The lightning on the spiraling arms of the storm bespoke the violence of the night.

Fine — I would ride the hard winds. I continued with my wide curves, circling a few kilometers away from the cliff face that hosted our shack and Mox. I hoped he would be okay, play it easy and slow, a bit stupid. Neither Core nor House would care anything for him.

And hopefully he would forgive me someday for keeping things from him.

With that thought, I expelled the last of the air from my lungs and accelerated my descent.

A few hundred meters above the clouds, my sky-surfing was interrupted by a coruscating bolt of violet lightning.

From *above* the storm.

"Inertia," I hissed as I snap-rolled into the crackling ionization trail from the shot, a near miss from an energy lance. With a quick scan of the sky above me, I saw a pair of black smears shooting by. Interceptors, from Hainan Landing, running on low-viz. Somebody wasn't waiting for me to come in.

Gravity and damnation: I didn't have anything that would knock down one of those puppies. I slipped into another series of rolls. None of their targeting systems would lock on me — not enough metal or EM, and I was moving too slow for their offensive envelope — so it was straight-line shots the old-fashioned way, with eyeball, Mark I, and a finger on the red button.

The human eye I could fool, and then some.

They circled over the storm and made another pass toward me. I kept spinning and rolling, bouncing around like a rivet in a centrifuge. *Think like a pilot, Vega.* I spilled air and dropped straight down just before both lances erupted. The beams crossed above me, crackling loud enough to be heard over the roar of the storm below.

It took some hard pulling to grab air out of my tumble. I

regained control just above the top of the storm, a close, gray landscape of thousands of voids and valleys, glowing in the light of the rising moon. It was eerily quiet, just above the roil of the clouds. The background roar I felt more in my bones than heard with my ears, like a color washing the world; the detail noises were gone — all the little crackles and hisses and birdcalls that fill a normal night. The only other sound was the periodic body-numbing sizzle of lightning bolts circling between cloud masses within the storm.

I had no electronics except the silicon stuffed inside my head. If I got hit hard enough to fry that, there wasn't going to be much future for me anyway. But those clowns on my trail had a lot more to lose from Mother Nature's light show than I did. So I cut a wide spiral, feinting and looping as I went, trying to draw them down closer to the clouds. They came after me, in long circles nearly as slow as their airspeed would allow, the two interceptors snapping off shots where they could.

It was a game of cat and bird. When would they fire? When should I weave instead of bob? I'd already surrendered almost all my altitude advantage. I didn't want to drop into the storm winds until I was close to my target, not if I could help it. My greatest problem was that I was muscle-powered. I couldn't keep this up nearly as long as my attackers could.

Then one of them got smart, goosed up a few hundred meters for a diving shot.

Gotcha. I rolled slow to give him a sweet target.

My clothes caught fire from the proximity of the energy lance's bolt. I twisted away, relying on the flames to take care of themselves in a moment, praying for my knowledge of the storm to pan out.

It did. Multiple terawatts of lightning clawed upward out of the clouds, completing the circuit opened by the energy lance's ionization trail. My bogey took enough juice to fry his low-viz shields and probably shut down every soft system he had. Regardless of its ground state, there's only so much energy an airframe can handle. Number one clown might not be toast, but he had too much jam sticking to him to be chasing me anymore.

Number two got smart and dropped below me, skimming in and out of the cloud tops. I guess he figured on there not being much more air traffic here tonight. I watched him circle, angling for an upward shot. Angling to draw the lightning to me.

Time for the clouds, Vega.

I folded my buckyfiber and dropped away from violent death, a bullet on the wing.

※

The storm was hell. Two-hundred-kilometer winds. Hail bigger than grapes. Sparks crackling off my wingtips, off my fingers, off my toes.

I loved it.

I had no idea where number two interceptor was, but he couldn't have any better idea where I was, so I figured that made us even. Neither House nor Core was going to find me down here. And to hell with the Governor-Generalship.

I was still a hundred kilometers or more from the probe, my real reason for being here. In the storm, I could steer — a little — and ride the winds — a lot. But it was like being inside a giant fist.

The training of my childhood came back to me, hard years in dark caves and abroad on moonless nights, initiating trickle mode. I could breathe as little as once every ten to twelve minutes when my blood was ramped up. The tensile strength of my skin rose past that of steel, shattering the ice balls when they hit me.

There's a beauty to everything in these worlds. A spray of blood on a bulkhead can be more delicate, ornate, than the finest hamph-ivory fan from Vlach. A shattered bone in the forest tells a history of the death of a deer, the future of patient beetles, and reflects the afternoon sun bright as any pearl. Take the symmetry in the worn knurl on an oxygen valve, the machined regularity of its manufacture compromised by the scars of life until the metal is a little sculpture of a tired heaven for sinning souls.

But a storm . . . oh, a storm.

Clouds tower, airy palaces for elemental forces. During the day, the colors deepen into a bruise upon the sky, and now, at night, they create the only color there is in the dark. The air reeks of electricity and water. Thunder rumbles with a sound so big I feel it in my bones. The blue flashes amidst the rainy dark could call spirits from the deep of the Big Ice to dance on the freezing winds.

I flew through that beauty, fleeing my pursuer, racing

toward whatever was consuming our number one probe.

※

The Houses aren't places, any more than Core is. They're more like ideas with money and weapons. Maybe political parties.

Powys House, as constituted on Hutchinson's World, was spread through several wings of the Governor-General's Palace of late lament. I had grown up occasionally visible as a page in the G-G's service. Between surgeries, training time, and long, dark hours in the caves of Capitol Massif.

Core is everywhere and nowhere. The Houses are nowhere and everywhere. Some believe there is no difference between Core and House, others that worlds separate us.

I spent my childhood falling, flying, being made both more and less than human.

I spent my childhood training for a day such as this.

※

Down below the cloud deck, I traded the storm's beauty for the storm's punishment. Here there was nothing but flying fog, freezing rain, ice, and wind — wind everywhere. It was brutally cold, frigid enough to stress even my enhanced thermal-management capabilities.

Screw you, Core. If that other bastard behind me made it to the Big Ice in one piece, I would give him a cold grave.

Then a gust hit me, a crosswind powerful enough to flip me with a crack of my wing spar and drive me down on to the Big Ice headfirst. I barely had time to get my arms up before I plowed through a crusted snow dune into a frigid, scraping hell.

"Damn," I mumbled through a mouthful of ice. That wasn't supposed to happen, not with these wings. The neurochannel control blocks screamed agony where the connections had ripped free on impact. I shut them down and began the wiggling, painful process of extracting myself. After a couple of minutes, I pulled free to see a pair of cold-foxes watching me.

"No food today," I said cheerfully over the howling wind, for all the good it would do me. Cold-foxes are long-bodied, scaled scavengers — and deaf. They eat mostly white-bugs, lichen, and each other; but at forty kilos per, they could be troublesome.

Something changed in the tone of the wind, and I looked

up in time to see the second interceptor roar by overhead, shaking on the wings of the storm. The cold-foxes vanished into the snow.

The Big Ice is shaped more like a desert than an ocean of ice, with dunes, banks, and troughs formed in response to the permanent storm. There are some density variations, relating mostly to aeration of the ice formations, but also trace minerals and pressure factors. The surface even has features mimicking normal geology — outcroppings, cliffs, crevasses. The difference is that geology sticks around for a while. The Big Ice . . . well, it has tectonics, but at human speeds rather than planetary.

Which for us mostly meant there'd never been much point in making or keeping maps. Every day was an adventure, down in the pit of the storm.

I was within a few kilometers of my instrument package's tunnels. The entrances would be filled with snow, possibly blocked by falls, but as long as at least one was open, I was in business.

I wasn't here only to avoid Core or whoever was after me — I hadn't lied to Mox when I told him I was a planetologist. The mystery of the Big Ice fascinated me, belonged to me, was mine to decipher and share, so much more important to me than Powys House and politics and Core. My brother would never understand.

And then I was sliding and struggling for footing against the wind, vehemently cursing what fascinated me.

The tunnel was a surprise when I found it. The number one probe had trundled across the Big Ice to this point, though its tracks had long been erased by wind and storm. As its entry point, it had chosen a solid cliff facing leeward, the closest thing on that particular stretch of the Big Ice to a permanent feature. The ice had preserved a tunnel like a black maw in the pale darkness.

I experienced a sudden shiver that had nothing to do with the temperature. At least I'd be out of the wind.

To access the tunnel, I had to get down on my hands and knees. It was almost like slithering, making me wish House had given me some genetic material from ice-worms. The tunnel was shaped in the slightly off-center ovoid cross section of the number one probe's body, the ice had melted, then injected into the walls to refreeze in denser spikes that served to reinforce the tunnel. Half-crawling, I had some clearance for my back, though not much. Were I to lie flat, I would barely have enough room to operate a handheld. Otherwise, it was a coffin of ice.

Hopefully I could prove deadlier than whatever might actually be inside the Big Ice.

To see, I had to use low-wave bioflare. It hurt my planetologist's soul, but I didn't want to be surprised by anything before finding the probe.

It was damned cold in the tunnels. My thermal management was keeping up, mostly due to the blessed lack of wind beyond a slight updraft from below, probably stimulated by some version of the Bernoulli effect at the tunnel mouth.

And if I had been merely human, the cold and the dark probably would have slain me with despair and hypothermia.

Stray voltage and a faint trace of machine oil led me to the probe. I approached cautiously, not sure what awaited me, what had sabotaged the probe.

In all the history of Core and House and humanity as a

whole, no one had ever found an alien machine. There were worlds that showed distinct signs of having been mined, or worked for transportation routes and widened harbors. But never so much as a rivet or a scrap of metal to be found: no machines, no artifacts.

And so we scoured the odd places for odd genetic signatures. Though as the centuries of Core raveled onward, it had become increasingly clear that the oddest genes were in our own cells.

Finally I found the number one probe, quiescent but not dead, and no evidence of what had savaged it.

The probe was vaguely potato-shaped, a meter-and-a-half wide by a meter tall in cross section and three meters long, with a rough surface studded with the bypass injectors that had created the tunnel. From the rear, it looked normal. No sign of the attacker. Just me and the probe, four hundred meters below the Big Ice.

Had our telemetry been spoofed? The trick was as old as Tesla's ghost, but the probe was stopped. That was more than spoofed telemetry.

I shut down, slipping into passive recon mode. Black.

Dampened my EM signatures, turned off my thermal management. Nothing but me and my ears on all their glorious frequencies.

The Big Ice groaned and cracked, settling into the rotation of the planet, the stresses of the crustal formations around and beneath it, breathing, a frigid monster half the size of a continent.

But there was something beyond that.

The gentle slide of crystals on crystals as the walls of the tunnel sublimated.

The distant echo of the storm.

A very faint click as something metallic sought thermal equilibrium with its surroundings.

And out of that near silence, a voice.

"Good-bye, Alicia." My brother Henri.

As fast as I was, he was faster. I was buried in tons of the Big Ice almost before I could even finish the thought: *sororicide.*

※

"House cadets are typically killed in their twelfth or thirteenth year of life. Appropriate measures are taken to preserve the brain stem and other structures critical to identity maintenance and retention of their extensive training. They are then left in a state of terminality until new training is called for. This process is considered critical to the development of their character, and since the dead know no flow of time, their thanatic interruption is not experienced by them as such. Some House cadets have waited centuries to be revived."

House: A Secret History in Fiction, (author unknown), quoted by Fyram Palatine in *A Study of Banned Texts and Their Consequences*, Fremont Press, Langhorne-Clemens IIa.

※

I found myself, reduced in cognitive ability, packed in loose snow.

Which meant I wasn't embedded in ice.

I have cavitation-fusion reactors within the buckyplastic honeycomb of my long bones. This means, given any meaningful thermal gradient at all, I will have energy. Even for exceedingly small values of thermal gradient. Such as being adjacent to a three-meter mass of plastic and metal, deep below an ice cap.

And given energy, the bodies of House, like the bodies of Core, will seek life. Repeatedly.

But if I was no longer buried in the ice, how long had I been here? My internal clock refused to answer.

Inertia.

I hadn't reached this state overnight. A cold stole over me that had nothing to do with the Big Ice. I could have been down here for months. Years even.

Then I realized I could hear the wind, close, which meant I was just below the surface. I had some muscle strength, so I pushed toward the noise. And if I heard noise, I had ears.

Above the rushing sound of the wind came some kind of long, drawn-out wail, not natural. With the part of my brain which was re-forming, I identified it as a siren.

Warning? Or call?

With my internal clock nonfunctional, I had no idea how long it took me to emerge from the snow, but eventually I did, body changing with my progress. There I found I could see.

I was at the base of a shallow hill — the cliff where the probe had tunneled? Worn by time and wind? How long had

I been beneath the Big Ice?

The siren wailed once again above the white expanses, and I followed it, climbing frozen wastelands.

With hands that weren't human.

I stopped, staring at the thing that had once been a palm with fingers. Now it was a claw, the skin a blue-fired tracery of webbing no human genome had ever produced. I had regrown myself from the stray organics down beneath the Big Ice.

The mysterious archaeogenes were within me.

And then another sound, a shot, followed by pain and a giant roar that wrenched itself out of my gut.

Mox stood above me, tranq gun poised, his expression bordering on terror.

I felt a surge, a burn of some strange emotion, retaliation, vengeance, but I fought it back, allowing the tranquilizers to work, staring at Mox, willing him to understand.

How could I make him realize that the monster in front of him was me?

※

I came to in a room in our shack, my hands and feet tied

with rudimentary restraints I knew wouldn't hold. Mox sat across from me, tranq gun across his lap, still looking scared and dazed.

Some primal impulse wanted to break my bonds and him, too, for trying to restrain me; but the part of me that had once been human was able to retain the upper hand.

I tried to speak, but all that emerged was something resembling a roar. Mox started up, gun trained on me.

I tried again. This time at least it was recognizable as speech.

"Planck on a half shell, Mox. Put down the gun." It was my quietest voice, but it reverberated off the walls of the little shack.

Mox winced and dropped the tranq gun. "Vega?"

I nodded; the less I spoke, the better.

"What happened to you?"

I shrugged. "The archaeogenes."

"But how?"

"House."

House was hard to kill. I had metabolized ice.

Mox nodded. He'd seen the data on the stray biologicals, too, and he thought I was a superwoman. He accepted it. He believed me.

The beast in me quieted.

"Now what?" he asked.

"Take me to Hainan Landing."

※

It had been over a year since my disappearance, and my brother Henri was now G-G. Core.

Unkillable?

"I did my research after you disappeared," Mox said. "Killing siblings is regarded as necessary to advancement among your kind."

"I was no competition," I roared. I wished there were something I could do about my beastly voice.

Mox winced, shaking his head. "Even if you assumed you'd taken yourself out of the running, he didn't assume that."

I don't know how I thought I could ever get away from House politics.

Since Mox had originally been ordered to bring me in before I went to find the probe, we decided that was what he would do — arrest me and take me to Henri. That would be the simplest way to get me to a place where I could confront my brother. There was a surge of that emotion again, the one I associated with the beast, a cross between anger and a powerful sense of ritual, like I imagined formal vengeance might once have felt.

Of course, the risk was that he would kill me on sight, but I was willing to take it. Besides, knowing Henri, he'd be curious to find out how I survived.

He would *want* to see me.

The transporter was a tight fit — it was made for two humans, and I had become very much bulkier.

As we flew over Hainan Landing, I inspected the changes. Capitol Massif was a mountain of rubble spilling into what was left of Mad Dog Bay. The city itself didn't look much different, its white low-rises spread like ancient pyramids among an emerald jungle topped with birds and flowers, bucolic existence beneath the gentle, guiding hand of Core. Flatboats and pontoon villages still graced the waterfront — surely new since Capitol Massif had collapsed. That must have been quite a tsunami.

But not caused by an earthquake, I was certain of that

now. Until I saw the city, it had still seemed possible that Henri had capitalized on a natural occurrence to further his ambitions.

Only too much of Hainan Landing was still standing.

Interceptors filed into formation with our transporter and accompanied us to the landing pad of what I presumed was the new palace, on the other side of Mad Dog Bay from the remnants of Capitol Massif and in a geologically stable location. A squad of heavy infantry was waiting when we stepped out of the vehicle, me with my clawed hands bound behind my back for verisimilitude. They formed up around us and led us through hallways even more convoluted than those I remembered from childhood.

Perhaps House really could become Core.

Then the hallways gave way to a huge audience chamber, paneled in mirrors to make it seem even bigger, and I was confronted by image upon image of what I had become — huge, ungainly, webbed, blue. Inhuman. Ugly as sin and more dangerous. How had Mox been able to converse with me as Vega? Look into my eyes and see the woman who had once been his lover? The sight of me scared even me.

But then there was my brother, standing at the end of the large room, hands locked behind his back, his stance mirroring my own bound wrists. Except that he still had the deliberately chiseled features of House: a look determined to provoke admiration, a look calculated to command. While I was something Other.

Beauty and the Beast.

Henri looked from Mox to me and back again. "*This* is supposed to be my sister?" he asked, one finely sculpted eyebrow raised for effect.

"Henri!" I roared before Mox had a chance to answer. My voice shattered the mirrors lining the hall and made my brother finally look at me seriously.

Henri shook his head. "This does not look like Alicia to me. Your humor is in poor taste."

The sense of formal vengeance surged, and I growled, causing everyone, including Mox, to step back.

Mox caught himself first. "Just talk to her."

"This could not have once been a human being."

"I think she reconstructed herself out of the archaeogenes in the Big Ice."

"But what is there in this — thing — to make you think it's her?"

"Planck on a half shell!" I bellowed, tired of being ignored. "Henri! Why?" It was all I could do to keep from breaking my bonds and tearing my ostensible brother to shreds.

Henri winced with everyone else in the hall at the sound of my voice, but now he was looking at me rather than Mox, accepting my transformation, recognizing me by my words if not my voice or my appearance. The calculating smile of House began to curl his lips.

No, not House. Core.

"Politics," Henri said, as if that explained everything. Which, of course, in terms of Core it did. "You were supposed to stay dead down there."

"Well, I'm back now," I said. More glass exploded. Was my voice growing bigger, or only my anger?

Henri actually laughed. "Yes, but bound."

This time I couldn't control the surge of emotion, and I snapped the buckyplastic bonds as if they were twine. Half a dozen guards stormed me, but I reached out one long, clawed arm and slapped them away, surprised at my own power. One guard began to rise, his weapon trained on me, but I broke his back and left him howling on the marble floor. I would have broken more, but then I saw the way Mox was looking at me, his expression even more horrified than the first time he had seen me.

"Halt!" Henri cried out, uselessly; by this time, no one was moving except the screaming soldier.

He approached me and stopped, facing me at arm's length. "As you look to be quite difficult to kill, sister, I have a proposal to make."

I could slay him before anyone shot me, I knew it — arm's length was not nearly distance enough for his safety. The being I had become calculated the speed and distance and moves without even thinking, and I kept this form's inherent need for formal vengeance in check only through the greatest effort.

And the awareness in my peripheral vision that three of the soldiers still standing had moved closer to Mox, weapons ready.

I had not moved my head, but I saw somehow that Henri

was cognizant of my assessment of the situation, knowing in the same way that I knew exactly how to break his neck.

"Proposal?" I echoed.

Henri smiled, sure of himself — Core. "I could use a creature like you at my side, you know. You would make a fearsome bodyguard. And you are no threat to my ambitions now . . . like this."

Like this. A monster, no longer House. What I had always wanted — but not *like this.*

"I might kill *you*," I bellowed.

He shook his head. "No. Because you, too, are Core. Sister."

"I'm not Core."

His smile grew even wider. "What then?"

Yes, what? A killing machine, obviously. And I could kill my brother — who, after all, had killed me first — kill him, and free Hutchinson's World of Core.

Two aides hurried in and loaded the wounded guard onto a stretcher. The man's screams faded to whimpers as they hauled him away.

In the moment of departure, I could scent everyone. The

wounded man's blood and pain and bodily fluids, Henri's brittle confidence, and fear everywhere. They were all scared — Mox, the guards, even Henri. Everyone was scared of the beast I had become.

What was underneath the Big Ice? What was so dreadful, so powerful, it had to be buried in such a huge grave?

Me. Something like me.

Did it have a conscience? Did *I* have a conscience?

I turned that thought over in my head. I was big, powerful, House-trained, angry — and back from the dead. I could challenge Henri here and now on his own ground. Somewhere inside me, that sense of formal vengeance stirred again. Some actions were *fitting.*

I gave that thought long consideration. Slow as the Big Ice, I turned it around and around. Some actions were fitting, but some actions were not.

Perhaps Core was not such a bad thing after all. And, as Henri had pointed out, if House Powys had become Core on this planet, then I, too, was Core — albeit monstrous Core now. But Core or not, I couldn't stay here, where I would likely kill anyone who crossed me. I *could* be better than whatever the Big Ice's archaeogenes had made me, better than what House had made me.

I could be better than my brother. I could be more than the sum of my biology. I did not have to accept his offer.

"I will not be your bodyguard."

My brother's smile disappeared. "Then I will have to kill you again, you know."

That he might. But what choice did I have? And how successful would he be this time? I looked at Mox, whose fear of me seemed to have fled. He held my gaze a long moment, and I imagined I saw some flicker of our old companionship.

Mox understood. And for his sake, I had to go.

I glanced once more at Henri. "I am not Core, and I never will be. Dead or alive, that will not change." I turned, expecting energy lances in my back.

Henri surprised me. None came.

I walked through the shards of shattered mirrors and down the long corridors and out of the New Palace, walked down to Mad Dog Bay and into it, walked beneath the waters and across the face of the land for days until I got home to the Big Ice.

Broad, deep, a world within a world. My place now. My family, my House. My Core. Perhaps if I dug deep enough, I could find a new brother.

END

The Rivers of Eden

Gleaming monitors displayed DNA recombinance in false-color animation. Adenine, thymine, cytosine and guanine. There was a hypnotic, mechanistic elegance to the rippling strands.

"The four-fold dance flows like the rivers of Eden," said Dr. Sarahbeth Mitchell, her head bowed as was proper.

"Pison, Gihon, Hiddekel, and Euphrates." Elder Joe McNally's voice resonated with a deep East Texas accent. "Each rising from the wellspring of existence. Each flowing into the ocean of life." His fleshy lips slipped into a smile not echoed in the droopy folds around his pale eyes. "Not unlike faith itself."

"Not unlike faith itself," she repeated.

To hell with faith and to hell with McNally. At least she had her work — including the work she concealed from her sponsors. She had often wondered about the wisdom of her decision to join the Davidites in order to avoid the Caliphate, but soon, very soon, her work would make them both history.

The Elder clasped his hands behind his back and rocked on his heels in a imitation of reflectiveness. "Have you ever wondered why we have both faith and free will, Miss Mitchell?"

That was a joke — the only free will left in the world was distributed among those immune to or uninfected by the *Tawhid* plague. Not to mention that McNally was totally uninterested in the free will of others: his project, dancing there on the screens in front of them, was a new plague, one that would reimprint the temporal lobes, sabotaging the Establishment in favor of the message of Christianity. A complex problem, on a par with the *Tawhid* plague itself, with the added difficulty of improving the meme-bombs so that they launched imperatives rather than suggestions. McNally's plague of faith was to be reinforced with strong social messages, calling Christians from their underground bunkers and remote compounds in a holy tide of arms controlled by McNally himself.

And making the whole world like this hell where she dwelled, this fundamentalist enclave on the fringes of the New Islamic World Order.

"As a simple woman, it is not given to me to think on questions of religious philosophy," she said.

McNally chuckled. His shiny black shoes moved out of her line of vision as he began to pace the lab. "I didn't mean the masses out there, you know — I meant those like you and me, the ones who can still make decisions. The ones who can change the course of the world."

"I would not presume, Elder." But of course she would. There were plagues and there were plagues, and McNally wasn't the only one who wanted one from her. Her progressive contacts in the Islamic underground outside the compound wanted a plague that attacked the temporal lobes and rewrote the mental software of faith back to a simulacrum of old-fashioned religious free will. Undoing the biological chains of the *Tawhid* plague and undermining the Establishment, but retaining the power and virtues of faith.

Sarahbeth had other plans. Her plague would do away with them all — the Davidites, the Caliphate, the world as a reflection of God's word. If He existed, surely He had not meant His creation to come to this. Then let people find faith in the light of reason, if it was there to be found. Sarahbeth doubted that very much.

She had developed a modified coronavirus sufficiently distinct from the wild versions to avoid existing immunities, then built on some of the original Lebanese programming from the *Tawhid* plague for her own work. She had over two thousand strains, all tested in high-resolution emulation of the human body and brain.

Now she needed a human test subject.

The sound of McNally's footsteps stopped behind her as he laid his meaty hands on her shoulders in a gesture which could be interpreted as friendly, but which she knew was not. "With our free will, we are the ones who can act as God's agents," he murmured close to her ear.

Sarahbeth forced herself not to squirm. "In faith, Elder."

On the monitors, gene sequences continued to flow in

twinned spiraling streams, the four rivers of Eden transforming into a wavering, particolored snake.

All this Eden needed now was an apple.

※

Norman Patenaude watched eagerly through the window as Dr. Sarahbeth Mitchell walked across the square of the former Baylor University campus. Her head was meekly lowered as befitted a modest woman, her dark skirt swinging around her calves. She was easily twice his age, but there were few women in the compound as pretty.

Luckily, he was saved from the sinful thoughts teasing him by the ring of the duty phone at his elbow.

"Sons of David," Norman said in English — God's language. "It's a great day in the firm hand of the Lord." Then, in Arabic, "*How may I serve you, God willing?*"

"*Praise be his name,*" responded the caller, also in Arabic. Norman felt his stomach tighten, in a different way than it had at the sight of Dr. Mitchell. The Davidites were tolerated by the Emirate of Texas and Oklahoma, but that did not change the fact that Norman's parents had been killed during the Establishment Wars, fighting the Muslims in the Battle of Baton Rouge.

The caller switched to English. "Hello Norman. How's the God business today?" It was Billy Mahmoud Finnegail, director of security for the Emirate in Waco. The Caliphate might tolerate the Christian enclaves, but they kept close tabs on them nonetheless.

"Same as ever," Norman said.

"We've had some reports of interesting activity among the Davidites," Billy said casually. "Does the phrase 'Rivers of Eden' mean anything to you?"

If he waited too long before answering, he would give himself away. "No, sir." Bearing false witness was a sin, even unto the enemies of the Lord; nonetheless, he deliberately paused for consideration, as he had been trained during his three years with the Security Deacon before he joined Elder McNally's personal service. "I mean, Genesis 2, I guess. Like in the Koran too." *Now pause for puzzlement.* "Should it mean something?" *He was innocent of incorrect thought or wrongdoing.*

Billy laughed. "I was asking you, Norman. *Peace.*"

※

Sarahbeth sat alone in the unmarried women's refectory,

eating a Granny Smith. The crisp flesh of the apple melted on her tongue with a bracing sourness laced with sweet, making her smile. It was almost midnight, and most of the chairs were stacked on the tables. Food banks blinked and hummed along one wall, and the lights were already dimmed.

Another bite, and she found the pip she'd been looking for. A hair-fine filament curled from one end. Sarahbeth dug it out of the apple and slipped it into the mesh covering her hair, tucking back a stray strand in case anyone was watching from the shadows of the refectory.

The familiar current pulsed from her hairnet into her cerebral cortex, gold-bearing complex organic molecules embedded in her glial cells serving as an antenna. The template for the engineered molecules had originally been deposited there by a transient virus. The signal was picked up and routed by the pirate neural chain to a bioprocessor the size of a rice grain, itself a carefully engineered growth-limited cancer introduced by yet another virus. The bioprocessor assembled the signal into sensory inputs, which were then injected into her Wernicke's area and the corresponding regions of her visual cortex.

"My friend," said her handler, an anonymous woman who always wore a *burqa*. The garb made Sarahbeth want to shudder, but her handlers were able to manipulate her flow of supplies, and so she played along with their wishes. And when it came right down to it, the *burqa* was less threatening than the hair net and the long skirts she was forced to wear here in McNally's tiny empire.

The language the woman spoke seemed to be English, though with the symbolics of preprocessed speech, that wouldn't have to be the case. Sarahbeth used to fear embedded programming, having her brain hacked, but once she realized that McNally hacked her consciousness on a daily basis without benefit of cutting edge biotech, it had become the lesser of two evils.

Her handler continued. "We have grown concerned about your recent reticence. Inbound resource shipments suggest that matters will soon be resolved. This cannot be tolerated without authorization. If you do not contact us, extreme measures will be taken. In four days, seek an orange with three scars on one end."

The woman flickered and was gone, subsumed into the

shadows of the refectory.

Sarahbeth stared at the spot where the image had disappeared. Somehow, her handlers had noticed that she was not playing entirely by their rules, probably by doing pattern analysis on the biologicals coming into the compound. Lately, Elder McNally had been stocking up on culture bases, preparing to go from experimental development to full-scale production. He had clever men responsible for burying the details of her work in a flood of random orders for related genetic feedstock, chemicals, and equipment.

Apparently not clever enough.

Her contacts wanted their plague, and soon. But what would they do if they didn't get it?

She was almost ready; she could promise without delivering, and by the time her own plague hit the streets, it wouldn't matter anymore.

Sarahbeth pulled a Davidite-approved postcard from her bag. With an old-fashioned ink pen, she wrote a note to her sister — a note that would be read by her handlers as well, who would find hidden meanings in the loops and whorls of her wavering cursive. It was time for a little less reticence.

The rivers are ready to flow, her code said to those with eyes to read it.

※

It was hot, even hotter than usual for a summer in Waco. Norman Patenaude was off the phone shift for a change, and despite the heat, he had taken the mail he was supposed to censor out to the grounds to sit beneath a wilting pecan tree. After less than half an hour, he was already beginning to regret it. The high walls around the Davidite compound blocked any hope of a breeze, and the asphalt paths through the grounds softened and stank beneath the summer sun. The limestone walls and red tile roofs of the Spanish revival buildings wavered in the heat. Even the turkey vultures had found a place to hide, while he was here of his own free will, sweat running down his shirt and the nose-tingling stink of traffic hissing by on the other side of the compound wall.

Another dozen postcards, and he would go back inside. Postcards were only allowed to those in good standing with the Deacons — message on one side, address on the other. No envelopes to hide secrets from the Lord or the Security Deacon.

Two requests for interlibrary loans of books Norman had never heard of — *Fifth Head of Cerberus* and *Mysterious America*. Both sounded vaguely sinful. He set the cards aside for the Deacon to review.

Three pen-pal notes, each with the discreet green dot of the Outreach Deacon on the bottom left corner — those went into the outgoing bin. No one had yet been converted as a result of the writing campaign, but it gave the children something to do.

A note to someone's sister asking about her health, followed by a verse from Ecclesiastes: "unto the place from whence the rivers come, thither they return again." Norman flipped the card over.

Dr. Sarahbeth Mitchell. One of Elder McNally's "specials."

Norman didn't know what the "Rivers of Eden" project was exactly, but Dr. Mitchell worked on it, and it was important. Finnegail had said the words just yesterday on the phone. The Security Deacon had been mighty upset when Norman reported the brief conversation.

Now Dr. Mitchell was sending a message to the outside,

to the unsaved — talking about rivers.

Normally a verse from the Bible wouldn't have set off any alarm bells, but Finnegail had just mentioned the Rivers of Eden project. And now this. Norman knew he should take the card to the Security Deacon, tell him his suspicions, but he couldn't shake off the sight of Dr. Mitchell hurrying across the lawn the other day, meek and proud at the same time. He knew she didn't really believe. She was tolerated because she was special, one of those who did God's work *despite* her faith instead of *because* of it. Dr. Mitchell had been some kind of big deal professor before the Final American Establishment, and like a lot of women, she'd been terrified of the *burqa*, the Shariat, and all the evil stories about the Caliphate.

And now she was inside Elder McNally's walls for life. When the Female Accountability Decree had first been issued, Dr. Mitchell had signed herself over to the Elder's custody, desperate to avoid being forced into an Islamic marriage on the outside. He'd read all about it in her security file.

Norman liked to read the files on pretty women.

If he went to her with the card, would she be grateful? He knew what she would go through if he took it to the Security Deacon. No, he couldn't do that: he'd seen the sadness around her eyes when she was meek. Those lovely eyes didn't need any more occasions for sadness.

He slipped the card in his pocket and went looking for Dr. Mitchell.

※

Sarahbeth sat on a cedar bench protected from the heat by wild rose and mustang grape vines, contemplating the tailoring of viruses and the unfairness of life. Two decades ago when she'd been in graduate school, work on human subjects was forbidden to American researchers. With no such constraints, Indian and Lebanese biotech had rapidly outstripped that of the U.S. and Europe. Their leading edge technology had created the *Tawhid* plague in a gray market lab in Aleppo, Syria, and soon it had been exploited by the Caliphate. The Establishment Wars swept the world, the plague creating a sudden army of the faithful, and then came the 30th Amendment to the Constitution and America's joyful accession to the Shariat.

All because some true believers in the Middle East had played around with viral architecture — and no laws had limited their research.

"Dr. Mitchell?" A young man interrupted the useless thoughts, the past that couldn't be changed. At least she had a future to live towards.

She turned her attention to the pale-skinned redhead with the big ears. She'd seen him before, following Elder McNally around.

Sarahbeth bowed her head. "It's Miss Mitchell, sir." She would be dutiful; this close to the end of everything and the beginning of everything else, she must remain obedient.

"I'm not a 'si-sir,'" he stuttered.

She didn't raise her head. "You are a man grown." *Although little more than a boy.* "I am an unmarried woman. I owe you my obedience. How may I serve you ... *sir?*" To her chagrin, she couldn't resist that little pause at the end.

His feet shuffled on the pavement in front of her and she heard him gulp. "P-please look up. And call me Norman."

"That would be improper." Women did not look men in the eye when speaking; that had been drilled into her often enough by now.

"Please." He sounded almost desperate. In another time

and place, his post-adolescent urgency might have been amusing, even endearing, but here, now, he had McNally's ear.

Making him a loaded gun.

She looked up. "How may I serve you, Norman?"

The young man handed her something — the card to her sister. Her message to her contacts outside who were threatening extreme measures if they didn't hear from her.

If this postcard didn't get sent, her time was running out.

"I'm the mail censor this week," he said, his voice wobbling.

Sarahbeth forced herself to sound amused. "My sister's health is hardly a subject of apostasy."

"No, ma'am, I suppose not. It's just ..."

Repressing the guilt she felt at the gesture, she took Norman's hand in both of hers, glancing around first to be sure they weren't being watched. But the climbing roses and vines to either side protected them, keeping out the hot Central Texas winds and prying, zealot eyes.

She stroked his wrist with her thumb and saw him swallow. Given the way the rank-and-file Davidites were treated,

Sarahbeth was willing to bet Norman hadn't been touched by a woman since his mother last hugged him. "What is it you want, Norman?"

"Ma'am, I ... it's the Rivers of Eden, ma'am." His voice tumbled in a squeaky rush. "*They* know."

Her fingers tightened involuntarily around his hand, and it felt as if the saliva had magically disappeared from her throat. Who were *they*? She licked her lips. "I'm sure I don't understand ... Norman."

"Ma'am, I know it's a special project, you're working on it, the Security Deacon's furious because Billy Finnegail asked about it, and now you're sending mail about rivers outside right after that and there's been a security breach and there could be all kinds of trouble and I just wanted to see if you were okay." He took a deep breath.

"Norman." She dropped her head again, assuming the aspect of meekness while her grip tightened around his wrist. "I'm afraid." *At least that much was true.* "I need a man to protect me. What should I do?"

Her own skin crawled at her words, but Norman twitched so hard Sarahbeth wondered if he was close to orgasm. The celibacy imposed on the young Davidite men was a form of slow torture. Of course, women had it worse under their rule, but then, a woman did not have the moral integrity to be her own agent, ever — something on which the Davidites and the Caliphate were in whole-hearted agreement.

Sarahbeth fought back the bitterness she battled constantly just as Norman yanked his hand out of hers, his face red and his breathing heavy. "Ma'am, I can't approve this card, but I ... I can lose it."

At that, he turned, stumbling in his hurry to flee temptation, running off past the draggled row of pecan trees and into the nearest building.

Hers.

With a sigh, she followed him.

※

Norman burst through a set of double doors without seeing where he was going, fleeing his shame, the hot pounding of his heart and the sinful straining of his crotch. Dr. Mitchell had turned to him in need and sweet innocence, and he had responded with lust beyond any he had ever known.

He kept running, finally stopping halfway down the hall, and leaned against the wall, taking a deep breath. Here it was cool and dry, the opposite of outside.

Shoes squeaked on the tiles and he turned. It was Dr. Mitchell, drawing him to her like the sun drew a planet into orbit.

"This building is restricted," she said. "Do you think it's wise for you to be here?"

"I didn't think, I just ran." *From you.* His voice faltered. "My sm-smart badge. It allows access. B-because I'm on the Elder's staff."

"I know that." She sighed. Fingers brushed his shoulder then dropped away again. "But the things I'm working on in my lab are dangerous."

Norman didn't answer at first, his mind playing around what he knew, his face hot from the brief touch of her fingers. "You were immune to the *Tawhid* Plague." He remembered that from her file.

She nodded. "I caught the infection, but something didn't take."

"The plague didn't take for my mom and dad either," he

said. "They were killed in the Battle of Baton Rouge. Afterwards, my aunt sent me here and the plague died out." He looked into the doctor's eyes. "But that's what you're doing with the Rivers of Eden. Making a new plague. A Christian plague."

The doors of the building opened again, and Elder McNally entered with several of the Security Deacon's men, hard-eyed body-builders with bright smiles.

Norman and Dr. Mitchell started apart as if they had been locked in an intimate embrace. In his imagination, they had been, and the thought was as bad as the deed.

The elder stopped next to them, shaking his head. "Norman, I won't have you *distracting* Miss Mitchell."

Dr. Mitchell bowed her head. "Sir, this is my doing."

McNally gave an amiable chuckle. "I can't discipline *you*. The Lord needs your skills too much."

Norman's stomach twisted; McNally was quite capable of punishing *him* for his fantasies.

Or what if they had monitored the conversation? What if they were aware that Norman knew too much? He didn't want to think what would happen to him then.

"Leave him here," the doctor said, her eyes still respectfully lowered. "He will be patient zero. We've discussed the need for a human subject to confirm the simulations."

McNally smiled, shaking his head slowly, a gesture of disbelief. "I do declare, Miss Mitchell, sometimes I think the good Lord might have erred when He did not make you a man."

Norman didn't agree — Dr. Mitchell was perfect as she was. And now he would be near her as her patient zero, whatever that was.

"Give him a cot here," McNally said to one of the security men. "And take his badge. He doesn't leave this lab without my personal approval."

"Yes, sir."

McNally stared at Norman. "Pray on this son. Pray hard."

Then the Elder and his followers swept away in a tide of pale robes and dark linen suits, without a backward glance.

※

The next afternoon, Sarahbeth received a delivery she hadn't expected. Two kilos of chilled agar, several dozen test packets of varying grades of fertilizer, and a small brown envelope of seed.

She tore open the envelope. Sure enough, the seeds had the telltale filaments. Her postcard hadn't gotten through, and now her outside contacts wanted to talk.

Badly.

Norman lay on his cot, reading his Bible, paying her little attention for a change. She sat down on a stool in front of one of her lab benches, a notebook in front of her, and slipped one of the seeds into the mesh of her hairnet. There was the familiar pulse of current before her handler flickered into being.

The image of the woman in the *burqa* was noisy and the resolution lower than normal; they'd rushed the message.

"Since we have not heard from you, we must regard your situation as unstable. You will have to abort the work. Set a fire to the lab within forty-eight hours of receiving this message, large enough that the Waco Fire Department will respond. We will have colleagues on the fire crew who will try to find you and get you out. Otherwise, we will have to storm the compound."

And with that, the woman in the *burqa* was gone.

Sarahbeth leaned back, staring at the place where her messenger had been. Everything was moving too fast — her contacts were forcing her hand.

She swiveled in her chair to face the young man she had taken responsibility for. "Norman."

He looked up from his bible with a smile, his trust — love even — transforming his homely features. Sarahbeth repressed a sigh.

"Yes, ma'am?"

"It's almost time for you to be patient zero."

He put his Bible aside and came over to her, touching her elbow, gentle, shy. "That's my job now, isn't it?"

She nodded and rose. "Yes, it is." It seemed unfair that she had to use this trusting boy-man to carry out her plans, but taking fairness too much into account was how Western Civilization had gotten where it was today.

She went to the freezer banks and gazed at the vials, over a decade's worth of work.

132. What her outside contacts wanted. Induced low-grade fever, temporary amnesia followed by lassitude, then a shift in temporal lobe chemistry and a wipe of selected memory tags in the cortex and hindbrain. That variant essentially erased the effects the *Tawhid* plague and rebooted the software of faith, the routines in the human subconscious that responded to prayer and meditation with a sense of being touched by divinity.

384. What McNally wanted. Also induced low-grade fever, with seizures likely in eight to ten percent of the population. Then a boost to the software of faith, along with spreading Christian memes via mRNA meme-bombs of unparalleled virulence. Mandatory believers, at levels deeper than even the *Tawhid* Plague had managed.

599ß. Her virus. Her solution. Similar pathology to the other viruses. Plus the use of a different class of mRNA meme-bombs to entirely wipe faith from the human consciousness, replace it with rational processes and an open path to self-knowledge. No better, probably, than what had gone before, not in a moral sense, but 599ß was as close as she could come to restoring freedom of thought and belief to this world. Unfortunately, her virus had unstable side effects, including the possibility of retrograde amnesia going back ten, maybe even fifteen years.

599ß also had a completely false data trail, both in her lab notebooks and on the computer systems. Not that anyone from McNally's security team who had ever audited her had enough genetics to understand what they were reading.

Sarahbeth checked out one of her two vials of 599ß and set it in the fast-breeder. "You'll get your chance soon, Norman. I'm brewing up a test batch for you."

"What do I have to do?"

"Just wait for now."

He sat down again, still trusting, and she dialed the fast-breeder to maximum production.

※

Norman came out of the little toilet cubicle in the lab to find Dr. Mitchell watching him with a smile on her face. His breath hitched in his chest, and to his shame he could feel his face flush.

That smile didn't mean anything, he told himself. His heartbeat didn't listen. "Ma'am?" he said, his voice cracking like an old egg.

"It's time, Norman," she said.

His crotch strained, causing his blush to deepen.

"For you to be patient zero," she added gently.

"Oh." He sat down on his cot and crossed his legs, praying for the hard-on to go away. To distract himself, he gazed around the large room: the row of windows on one wall, the tables and racks of gleaming glassware, the metal stands and electronic test equipment, the cluster of monitors and computers at one end.

She perched next to him, tucking a swirl of her brown hair into her hairnet. She was so close he could feel her warmth, smell her female scent. Her breath stirred the tiny hairs on his right forearm. Dr. Mitchell took his hand and started rubbing his knuckles.

"A long time ago," she said, "when I was trained, we had —"

"Not that long ago, ma'am," Norman blurted.

She actually laughed at that, her hazel eyes bright and wide for a moment as her shoulders drew back and her chin came up. That was when Norman knew he loved Dr. Mitchell, not just with a sinful yearning of the flesh, but soul to soul. In the eyes of the Lord.

"Shhh," She touched her lips with one finger.

For a moment, he thought she might touch his, too.

"A while ago," Dr. Mitchell continued, "however long that was, we had a thing called 'informed consent.'" Now she looked sad again, with her usual frown and slumped shoulders. "That's been gone since the Establishment. But I'm something of a traditionalist."

"'Informed consent,' ma'am?" This time his voice didn't crack.

"That means I tell you what I'm going to do before I do it." She squeezed his hand. "Here in the lab, I mean."

"The virus."

"Yes." Dr. Mitchell looked at the floor, almost mumbling. "I need to infect a human, to see how it progresses outside the simulations."

He shivered. "What will it do to me?"

"Faith, Norman," said Dr. Mitchell. "Have faith. This will set you free."

"Kind of like the truth does, huh?"

"Ever wonder why the rivers flowed away from Eden?" she asked quietly. "Why would water flee perfection?"

Then Dr. Mitchell dropped his hand. She walked back to

her bench — that's what she called it, though it didn't look anything like a bench to Norman. There she sliced an apple and set it onto a tray along with a large syringe. She stood there, breathing, staring down at the tray for a while, then brought it back to him.

"Have some apple. " Dr. Mitchell slipped a piece into his mouth, her fingers brushing his lips, and he shuddered. Then she tugged his right sleeve up from his biceps almost to his shoulder, and swabbed his skin with alcohol.

He chewed the apple as she picked up the syringe. "Is this informed consent, Dr. Mitchell?"

"No," she said, and plunged the needle into his arm.

※

Patient zero developed a fever of 39.4 degrees within an hour of injection, Sarahbeth noted in her lab book early the next morning. *Patient has since stabilized slightly below 39 degrees. Seems to be resting comfortably. Introduced saline drip at 18:30 hours.*

She'd only needed to wait about eighteen hours until Norman entered the infectious stage. Though he was dozing, his nose had started running. He'd even sneezed twice already.

What she didn't record was that she'd spent part of the night on the cot with him, holding him, pretending ... what? That he was a son? A lover? She'd never had a child, and the few tussles she'd had with fellow students, grad students, and assistant professors before the Establishment of the Caliphate hardly qualified as the other. When she was young, she'd been too driven to devote enough time to a relationship, and now there was no opportunity. Not unless she fancied the prison of marriage, or being stoned as an adulteress.

So she'd held Norman while he moaned and tossed, hadn't pushed his hands away when he found her hips, not knowing what exactly possessed her. It certainly didn't feel like desire, but it did feel like tenderness.

And she had to smile when even in his sleep Norman twitched nervously as his hands strayed.

Now the sun had come, and with it, the rusty-hinge song of the grackles in the pecan trees outside her lab window, screeching the dawn of the first pulsing heat of the day. Bells tolled for prayer, for breakfast, for the first shift, all these bells, always demanding something of her. Beyond the walls, the *muezzins* wailed morning prayer as all traffic stopped and thousands of doors clicked open, thousands of people knelt in prayer on the roads and sidewalks, their clothes rustling and settling about them. She could hardly remember a time without bells and wails, and at the same time, that long-vanished blessed silence filled her waking dreams.

Sarahbeth turned and looked over at Norman. His pale complexion was flushed, and sweat generously graced his temples. She buried her face in her hands. What if something was wrong with her virus? What if there were adverse side-effects ... or Norman were killed? He was just a kid, he had no idea. Her virus was supposed to set him free, but did he need that?

She shook her head and rose. Fire. She had to set a fire. She had set the process in motion, but she needed outsiders to complete the circle, to be infected with her plague and spread it beyond the compound and far into the world with a message of individual moral responsibility.

Her contacts had said they would come for her disguised as emergency workers, but that was immaterial now. What mattered was the virus, sweeping north to Dallas and the plains beyond, and south across the hot Texas Hill Country to Austin.

Sarahbeth began to gather her lab notes, some shelf liner, a pile of paper smocks — anything that would burn. She built the pile on her lab bench next to the tray with the empty syringe and the withered brown apple slices. The door creaked open behind her and she turned.

Elder McNally. Alone.

"You never returned to your dormitory last night, Miss Mitchell," he said, raising his eyebrows. "Were you, ah, *training* your patient?"

Sarahbeth repressed the sharp retort she would have liked to throw at him and bowed her head. "I need to monitor his condition. He's in the mid-course of the infection."

"384, I trust?"

Her head shot up and she stared at McNally, her hands growing suddenly cold. Had she ever shared the viral family lists with him?

"I'm not such an idiot as you think," McNally said, as if she'd asked the question aloud. "The labels on the vials in your lab freezers are there for anyone to read."

She drew a ragged breath. "You have no idea what those different virus families are."

"Yes," the Elder said, "I do."

She gazed at him, unable to answer.

He stared back, storm-gray eyes calm as a prayer. "384 is the plague of faith, the plague that will bring light back into a world of darkness. The Rivers of Eden. Do you want to tell me what are the other two are?"

"Strains that didn't work out."

"And what will the results be if we test that?"

Once again, she had no answer.

McNally advanced on her with a graceless lumber, one heavy hand coming down on each shoulder. "I've always admired you, Miss Mitchell," he said softly. "I might be persuaded to be lenient in the matter of your attempted betrayal. To that end I've left orders we, ah, not be disturbed."

Her stomach roiling, she feigned acquiescence. "But what about Norman?"

His hands slid from her shoulders to her waist. "He's in the course of the infection, is he not? He won't notice."

Sarahbeth allowed her hips to be drawn forward until

her pelvis touched his. Pretending to support herself on the table, she reached behind her for the syringe. In one smooth motion, she brought it up and stabbed Elder McNally in the eye.

His scream could probably be heard throughout the compound; she would have to work fast. Ignoring the Elder where he lay on the floor of the lab, writhing and moaning, she pulled Norman up from his cot, and dragged him to the windows of the lab.

Norman groaned and put a hand to his forehead. "Huh ... Where am I? Who are you?"

Yes.

She tugged open a window. "A friend. And this is an emergency. You need to get away from this building."

He gazed at her blankly as she pushed him out into the bushes.

Muttering something strangely like a prayer, Sarahbeth closed the window again behind him.

One hand pressed to his eye, McNally was trying to get up as he cried and cursed. Sarahbeth snatched a ring stand off the lab bench, raised it high, and slammed the heavy cast-iron base into McNally's head. She hit him a few dozen more times just to be sure, and then threw up in the corner of the lab.

When she stopped gagging, she opened four gas jets one by one. "I name you Pison," she told the first jet. The next was Gihon, then Hiddekel, and finally Euphrates. At the last, she wiped away the tears streaming down her face with the back of her hand. "Flow, rivers of Eden, flow."

Luckily, there was still no sign of Security. Sarahbeth slipped down next to a silent, cooling McNally with the lighter in one hand and allowed herself the luxury of telling him in vivid detail exactly what she thought of him. She could barely breathe from the reek of the gas when she finally heard the sound of running, booted feet down the hall.

Sarahbeth smiled and clicked the lighter.

END

Visiting Bad Town

> "Visiting Bad Town is like a series of vicious kicks in the teeth."
>
> Dozois the Gardener

The port of Bad Town is for the truly adventurous at heart. Built around a cometary body orbiting the red giant Qualle-a17 (a class B2 star) it provides an interplanetary experience unlike any other. The vistas are unique, the city's atmosphere something you will never forget. If you are interested in visiting, be sure to inform the ship's purser upon boarding: the *WSFS Armadillo* only makes port at Bad Town when sufficient passenger demand exists and restraining orders have lapsed.

In the event that a stop has been scheduled, the casual tourist is advised to remain on board with the cabin's intrusion countermeasures set to "fatal" or higher. If you intend to venture forth, management recommends at least a Class IV munitions license with ranged energy weapons endorsement and appropriate armaments of your choice. It is also possible to hire off-duty crewmembers for escort duty, at their own risk and for a substantial fee.

As a free-floating city in a power-assisted cometary orbit, Bad Town experiences highly variable seasons. During close approach to Qualle-a17, Bad Town's methane ice cores flare and outgas in a spectacular show which the city's Tourism and Salvage Committee claims results in a fatality rate of just under eighteen percent. (Unfortunately, this particular attraction cannot be viewed during a trip with the *Armadillo*, as management prefers to avoid the port during approach.) In the immediate postperihelionic period, Qualle-a17's blood red light sets the duraglass towers of Bad Town sparkling with a luminance that the great poet Dozois the Gardener once described as "hell's own ruby lasers shining in my sweaty eye." Nearer to apohelion, methane sublimation and the city's gaseous exudations combine to form an astonishing lacework that interweaves the towers with, to quote Dozois again, "a glittering grace rarely seen outside the dreaming mind of God."

Bad Town's healthy economy has its basis primarily in a transcription error in the trade factoring clauses of the Third Treaty of Epsilon Eridani. As a result, unregulated time-compression futures and produce massing less than 800 grams per individual harvestable unit (IHU, as defined by the Treaty Authority's Trade Board) cannot be taxed within Bad Town's orbital jurisdiction. The corresponding gray markets control civic operations. Tourists should be aware that the classic New Old New Zealand Oxygen Scam (NONZOS) is frequent in Bad Town, but as it is operated by what serves as Bad Town's government, it cannot strictly be considered unlawful.

When visiting Bad Town, be sure to shop in the delightful Skank Quarter, where native handicrafts in imitation of a hundred worlds can be purchased alongside delicious freshly-roasted skewers of meat-related protein mass. Please note that upon re-boarding *WSFS Armadillo*, tourists who have breached oral-esophageal barriers will be required to remain in quarantine in the UV chamber for seventy-two hours.

Enjoy your stay in Bad Town! Should you choose to remain in your cabin in the case a stopover, pay-per-experience entertainment fees will be waived while in port.

END

Return to Nowhere

Clevis Blackburn looked down at the I-84 bridge over the Snake River. On his side of the river, the First Oregon Cavalry checkpoint was quiet, orderly, big trucks idling in a long line as bored troopers checked papers and inspected the undersides of trailers. As if anyone was going to sneak back *into* the United States.

On the other side, the Idaho side, the checkpoint was less organized, a muddle of pick-up trucks and rope lines and three or four competing militias arguing with each other and with the westbound drivers. It was "Real America" over there, as the huge banner strung from scraggly pines proclaimed from the east bank of the Snake. The town of Ramey spread out beyond, fire-blackened stretches of buildings reminding Oregon and the rest of the west coast of what the

Free States had fled the previous year.

Real America, alright, Clevis thought. He'd already survived one march to freedom. Only a madman would go back and try again.

Or a loving fool.

He figured himself for a madman.

"Come on," said the guide, a *coyote* who'd spent years running bored farm boys and frustrated students, as well as slaves and dissidents, across the northern border into Canada, back when there was a United States to flee. From there they would make the arduous journey across the Yukon to Russian Aleskaya. While the Canadians had been happy to turn a blind eye on the Underground Railroad to Russia and Freedom, they were economically interdependent with the United States and couldn't afford to harbor escaped slaves themselves.

Now, since the secession, the journey was much shorter, only to Washington or Oregon or California.

Even so, going the other way was a curious trip, the man had told him over an egg breakfast that morning, because no one ever wanted *in.*

They'd both pretended the *coyote* didn't know who Clevis was.

※

A magazine cover. *The Economist*, out of London. Though England is a political and military backwater, Albion still plays hosts to some of the finest analysts and educators Old Europe has to offer.

There is a photo, digitally morphed and mosaiced into something like a cross between a Flemish masterwork and the tiling in a Roman bath. It is an image of a homely black man with a lazy eye and a missing tooth, rendered majestic by the magic of an ex-pat Japanese art director and the miracle of Photoshop. The headline reads: *The Last Slave in America.*

Clevis hates the picture, what it makes of him. He hates the headline more. If only it were true.

He is far from the last slave: there are still too many in the states that didn't ratify the Emancipation Proclamation, the states that had not seceded when it became obvious that the XXVIIIth amendment to the Constitution would not pass.

At least two of those slaves are still in the idyllically

named and idyllically situated Estes Park, Colorado — an old woman and a young child.

※

The *coyote* passed him a thermos as they sat with their backs to a pair of boulders on the east side of the river, out of sight of border patrols. The little Zodiac raft was well-hidden in a cottonwood break down by the water below them.

"You have those fake papers?" the older man asked.

Clevis patted his shirt pocket and took the thermos gratefully. "I'm prepared."

The *coyote*'s expression told him how little the smuggler believed that.

Clevis poured himself a cup of the strong, black coffee. "You forget that I know very well what it's like over here."

The other man looked away, his gaze catching on a tumble of salvia and creosote. He spat a wad of something mildly disgusting into the dust to the right of their feet and took back the thermos. "Nah, didn't forget. Just wanted to make sure *you* remember."

※

Mostly Clevis wishes he didn't have to remember. Remember what had happened to Doreen. Remember Lindy sick, too ill to travel. His child, leaving his child...

No.

But he had done it, had led hundreds of slaves disguised as tourists to Rocky Mountain National Park, over the mountain passes, through desolate areas of Utah and Idaho, to freedom in Oregon.

His wife is long dead.

But her child — their child — is alive.

And still a slave.

※

He walked the back roads toward Boise. The Interstate might have been faster, hitching with a trucker, but a lone black man in ragged clothes would be a far more ordinary sight on the two lane blacktop. Highway 52 to 16 to 44 and on down into the big city.

The underground railroad didn't run so well in reverse, but Clevis knew names and safe houses. He didn't need to be hidden away, not for this part of the trip, but he needed places to stay. Slave hunting wasn't the business it used to be, even back during the days of his childhood on the Colorado prairies, but there were still die-hards and bounty hunters looking for darkies heading west. The political failure of Emancipation had been largely symbolic — slavery had been foundering on economics for three generations.

Now, walking east deeper into slave country, he was nobody. A nobody with papers saying he belonged to a tech combine in Longmont, Colorado, and was authorized to return home after a long-term assignment doing militia tech support near the Blue Frontier. As long as one of the three or four people in Idaho who actually read *The Economist* didn't pass by, Clevis figured he was safe enough. Thank God the Red fetish for repressing slaves extended to a lack of photo ID.

It was already early fall, and Idaho was high enough in altitude to have that slight scent of winter. Clevis' hands ached, in the bones along the back of the palm, which told him cold was coming.

An old rust-colored truck with farm plates chugged past, then shuddered to a halt on the side of the road. A thin, tanned man with iron-gray braids leaned out the driver door and stared back at Clevis before shouting, "You looking for day work, boy?"

Clevis kept walking, shook his head. "No, sir. Heading home."

"Where's home, boy?"

Clevis got closer and realized that the driver was not white, but Indian. Free, in a sense. "Colorado, sir."

"Hmm."

They met eye-to-eye, the old Indian staring intently into Clevis' face the way no white man ever would have, except maybe a cop. "I got to run over to Pocatello tomorrow or the next day. Good sight closer to Colorado than here. You help me today, I'll give you that ride."

There wasn't a graceful way to get out of this, Clevis realized, and Pocatello was at least as far as he could hope to get in two days' walking and hitching.

"What kind of work?" he asked.

"A darkie, being fussy?" The Indian laughed. "Nothing that'll hurt your hands, Mr. Blackburn."

Clevis was in the truck before the Indian's use of his name registered. But the engine was rattling and the radio was blurting some twangy Red State standard, and they were off.

※

A photograph. Of darkies, which is rare. Most folks won't waste film on slaves, and they're not allowed identification. There's a couple with a baby, standing in a field with mountains behind them, flat and tiny in the photo, but from their shape those peaks must be tall.

Clevis remembers a fat white hand holding the photo. Folding it. Creasing it. Taking a lighter to it, and laughing when the darkie danced his agony.

He has trouble remembering his wife's face anymore. Like the photo, she is just an ashy blur to him now, a shape in the darkness that he still wakes up looking for after all this time. Clevis worries that someday he will forget her name, too, though he has never forgotten for a moment the blinding fire the love of her makes in his head and in his heart.

Fire. It always comes back to fire and flame.

※

In Pocatello, the Indian, Sam Edmo, dropped Clevis off at the intersection of Main and Center, an odd look in his eyes. But he had given Clevis no sign that he was with the underground railroad, and Clevis wasn't about to take the risk of betraying a safe house.

"I suggest you grow a beard," Edmo said. "Darkies may all look the same to white men, but some do look closer than others. And some even read foreign magazines."

Clevis nodded, but before he could slam the door of the truck, the Indian reached across the empty seat with a small, wrapped package, which he pressed into Clevis's hands. "Avoid Utah. And stop by Fort Hall next time you're in the area."

"Thank you, sir," Clevis said, closing the rust-colored door and stepping back.

He didn't want to open the package here at the busy intersection, so he walked a block on Center Street to Arthur Avenue and turned left. The western foothills of the Tetons loomed in the distance, and picturesque buildings from the previous century lined the street, but Clevis saw little more than the curious stares of the people who passed him.

Not enough darkies in this damned town.

A block before he reached the safe house, Clevis's steps slowed; even from this distance, it looked deserted, most of the blinds lowered despite the clouds in the sky. He turned left on Benton, back in the direction of Main, doing his best to appear unconcerned.

Was that an unmarked cop car down the street?

Clevis swallowed and forced himself to keep walking at a normal pace, when what he most wanted to do was break into a run. Pocatello wasn't safe anymore, and Sam Edmo hadn't known it either. If the Indian had meant him harm, he could have turned Clevis in himself and collected the reward.

Clevis had to get out of town, fast.

In the distance, a train whistle sounded, increasingly shrill as the train neared. The tracks were just blocks away — all he would have to do would be to find a freight heading for Wyoming.

But not Utah.

He picked up his pace, angling for the tracks, still trying to look casual for the cops who might be behind him.

A minute's walking brought the Northern Pacific coal train rattling past, hopper cars stretching in a line toward the short horizon. It was running empty toward the Wyoming mines, then. Even now, after secession, the Blue States and the Red States had interlocked economies.

If he lived so long, Clevis would find a way to end that, too.

The train was slow, moving at speeds respectful of Pocatello's dozens of grade crossings and massive switchyard. He glanced over his shoulder to see if the cops had followed him to the right-of-way. Then he ran, though it pained his ankles to scramble on the cinder ballast of the tracks.

No way Clevis would run as fast as the train, but he could run fast enough to snatch at a ladder without having his arm torn off. As long as he didn't stumble, and fall under the wheels, or get dragged by one of the hopper cars.

Then it was pounding feet and breath like hammers in his chest and one iron rung slipped by and here came the next and he leaned, grabbed and was jerked off his feet, nearly breaking his wrist as a bullet spanged off the metal of the car right in front of him.

Clevis twisted in surprise to see two men — cops? — pistols braced, trying to shoot him off the rail car.

It was a hopper car, with a little triangular space at the end behind the ladder, over the coupler. He ducked into the meager shelter even as the hollow metal rang with three, four more shots.

Out the other side? Or huddle? All they had to do was get in their vehicle, outrun the train, and call in to stop it.

He couldn't do anything about that. It would take several miles to halt the train, so once it started braking he would have time and places to jump.

Clevis stepped rearward, into the matching triangular shelter of the next hopper car. No more bullets drummed off the high metal sides. He swung out on the far side of the train from the shooters, scrambled up the short ladder, and rolled over the lip of the car, sliding down the riveted metal to jar painfully against the discharge doors at the bottom.

He didn't hear train brakes squealing.

Hopefully the blessed thing was going to Wyoming. He didn't recall any coal fields being worked in Utah. Copper and silver, yes, but the abundant black dust already smearing his clothes and hands testified that this was indeed a coal car.

After catching his breath and settling himself with a small prayer to the God who had long ago abandoned him, Clevis drew Sam Edmo's package out of his coat.

It was about the size of a book. Somewhat smaller and slightly thick. Though it appeared to have been wrapped for mailing, there was no address or postage on the outside.

He tore open the wrappings, prised apart the taped-together cardboard. Inside was old tissue, salvaged from some other purpose, wrapped around something small and relatively heavy.

When Clevis plucked off the paper, a medallion fell into his hand. He turned it over and over.

One side was stamped with the image of some building, surrounded at the rim by the words, "Boulder, CO Labor Exposition 2003".

The other side had a three-quarter profile of a woman, surrounded by the words, "Queen of Labor and Noble Service."

The face...

He dropped the medallion in his shock, then scrambled to recover it before it became wedged and lost in the hopper doors beneath his feet.

Memory rushed back to him, a storm of pain and regret. It was his wife's face — the blur vanishing like ash on the wind. As she might have looked if she'd lived these past five years, instead of rotting in a Colorado grave, body separated into pieces by a white man's axe in the name of posse justice.

"No," Clevis whispered, laying his head against the sloped side of the car. The rhythm of the rails made the metal vibrate, made his skull vibrate.

"No."

The engine whistled then, somewhere far ahead, the cars shuddered as the train began braking in earnest for a stop.

Here, the train tracks ran right next to I-15, probably the first place the cops would be looking for him. But on the other side was the Portneuf River.

Which was still his best bet.

The right side of the car then. He scrambled to the rim of the hopper car, keeping his head low, and waited for the train to slow down enough that the fall wouldn't kill him. At the earliest possible opportunity, Clevis slipped over the edge of coal car, tucked his knees up against his chest, dropped, rolled, and ran, hoping the face on the medallion wouldn't steal his purpose and his concentration.

He headed back in the direction of Pocatello, figuring the

search would be least likely there, following the river and hiding in the underbrush along the banks as much as possible.

He was in luck. After perhaps fifteen minutes crashing through bushes and trees when there was no one around to see it, and trying to walk casual when there was, he spotted a bridge ahead. None too soon. Behind him, in the direction of the Idaho border, helicopters circled in the sky above the stopped train, their orbits growing ever wider.

Helicopters for a runaway slave? The expense would be almost more than his value to the company that still officially owned him here in what was left of the United States of America, ostracized and morally corrupt superpower. He didn't want to think about what the helicopters meant, didn't want to think about the medallion in the pocket of his pants.

What he had to think about was Lindy, left behind with her grandmother in a safe house in Estes Park. Lindy, with her mother's strikingly hazel green eyes in her dark face and his own gaunt build — all achingly beautiful on her.

A girl for whom life as a slave would be a special kind of hell.

Clevis made the bridge without mishap and turned left, crossing as casually as he could manage, given the panic that was flirting with the edges of his mind and turning his stomach to knots. The road passed a scattering of buildings that claimed to be the town of Portneuf, luckily sleepy and unaware.

And ahead at the only intersection in sight, a rust-colored truck waited.

※

A shred of a newspaper clipping, undated and yellowed with age and creased with fold lines and wallet-grease, tacked to a cork board in a small town in coastal Oregon. The spidery, wandering hand of someone who learned to write as an adult has written in smudged pencil in the narrow white space along the side, "Estes Park Trail-Gazette." The other margin reads "C's 4rth grade gradyuashin." There's no photo of course, not on a column torn from the weekly "Colored Highlights" page.

followed by a performance that this reporter can only characterize charitably as unusual. One young man, Clevis Blackburn (of the county labor pool), recited the Declaration of Independence. It is always amazing to see a Colored person achieve always amazing to see a Colored person achieve such potential, even if only through rote memorization, though the nerve of the young man's teacher in allowing him to recite that particular document cannot be allowed to pass without remark. In a more seemly display of their own history, other youths in the Colored graduating class then demonstrated how a cotton gin could

※

Clevis clambered into the seat next to the Indian, hesitant, in fear of his life and his safety but needing the help. "Funny running into you here again, Mr. Edmo."

"Ain't it though?" The older man started the engine, peering into the sky. "Don't like the look of those helicopters."

"Neither do I."

Edmo gave a rustling noise that sounded vaguely like a chuckle. "Sorry about the misunderstanding back there in Pocatello. I thought you'd be taken care of."

Clevis nodded, smiling. If he was going to be trapped in a rust-colored pickup, there were worse people to be stuck with than Sam Edmo, with his gaunt poker face and dry humor and iron-gray braids.

The Indian turned the truck around and took the road south.

Clevis shifted uncomfortably, torn between the need for safety and the need for trust. "I thought you said to avoid Utah."

"Circumstances change." Edmo kept eyes on the road, as if pits were likely to open up and swallow the truck. "And the more immediate circumstances to avoid right now are those helicopters in the sky to the east."

※

A dark child runs through knee-high grass, chasing buzzing locusts that leap skyward fast and high as any toy his granddaddy ever carved. He laughs at the mountains around him, their heads as white as anything that is good and proper in life.

Jumping over old tires and the trash of three generations of his town, he runs past a straggled grove of trees and cannons off a white man who stands, legs apart, arguing with a darkie.

In little Clevis's experience, darkies never argue. They just say "yessir" and "nossir" and look at the ground a lot.

"...going to have to — " the white man is almost shouting, but stops to scoop up Clevis.

He's never been touched by a master before, and he begins to cry.

"Hey, hey, little man," says the darkie. It's someone Clevis recognizes but doesn't know, from over at the county. That slave comes to their church sometimes, and meets with the pastor and deacons after services while Clevis's momma ladles out punch and Clevis plays in the sanctuary away from the grown-up words. He reaches to take Clevis from the white man.

"No," says the white man, holding Clevis away from his body to meet the boy's eyes. "Listen, son."

Clevis shivers.

"There's no one here. Never been no one here. Never will be."

"Yessir," Clevis mutters.

"Future's coming, boy. Never forget."

Then Clevis is off and running, but now he knows he will sneak down to the tiring room and listen to those grown-up words. Listen for the sound of the future, though even at his age he knows it will mostly be bullets and dogs.

※

Clevis dozed, dreaming of his wife's face in places they had never been before, of fat white men striking out medallions in order to torment him, a darkie that half the world knew. He shuddered awake as the rhythm of the tires changed.

Edmo was exiting I-15 into a town called Virginia — pride of Bannock County. Clevis caught a glimpse of a sign for US-91 toward Logan, Utah.

He must have slept an hour or more. What was Edmo doing? Not selling him out, certainly.

"Why are you taking days out of your life for me?" Clevis was going the wrong direction, after all — the helpers dedicated to the underground railroad sent those who sought them out to the north or the west, now that Washington, Oregon and California had seceded. Or northeast, in those areas of the country closest to the states that had once been New England.

Sam Edmo gave that rustling noise again, that Clevis chose to think of as a chuckle.

"Mr. Blackburn."

"Clevis."

"Mr. Blackburn. You are nothing less than a legend in these parts. While I ain't devoted my life to The Cause, I know enough who have, and I know about you." Edmo's words were slipping deeper into a Red State pattern that stung exquisitely of old home and childhood. "Ain't so many of us would turn down a chance to participate in a legend. 'Specially not one we believe in."

Clevis dug the medallion out of the pockets of his pants. "And what about this?" Bitterness, unwanted, unneeded, crept into his voice. "Is this part of the legend?"

"Ain't got no idea what that's about, Mr. Blackburn." Edmo sighed, puffing out his cheeks. "It was give to me by Mi — someone, from the railroad." The old Indian took his eyes off the road briefly to glance sidelong at Clevis. "Someone. Who told me to watch out for you coming east. Wrong-Way Blackburn, they're calling you."

"And if it wasn't you that found me?"

"I reckon there's a million of them coins out there, Mr. Blackburn. They don't ever make just one or two."

He stared at his wife's profile. Someone wanted to make sure he didn't turn back. *Had they struck the entire series, just to get his attention?*

Not that he would ever turn away from Lindy. No matter what.

※

Edmo stopped the truck just south of Franklin, Idaho. He left the highway, followed a logging track into a stand of second-growth forest.

"There's checkpoints at the state line these days," the Indian told Clevis. "You could head east, for Wyoming, but I wouldn't without a good map and a local guide." He shrugged. "Which I ain't got either one of, sad to say." Edmo reached under the seat and pulled out a Big Chief tablet, like a schoolchild might have carried. "But I do have something for you."

He pulled down a ballpoint pen clipped to the truck's sun visor and began to write, with the quick, flowing script of someone who corresponded often and well. Clevis watched, fascinated. Words flowed from people and back to people, the true magic of the world. He wouldn't have picked Edmo to be such an enthusiastic user of pen and paper.

Edmo finished his note, signed it with a flourish, then dug in the glove box for a little leather sack. He pulled out a document seal and clamped it on the bottom of the tablet page, squeezing the handles with a clacking noise.

"Tribal notary," Edmo said with a grin, then carefully tore the page out and handed it to Clevis.

It was a handwritten ownership document, claiming Clevis as Edmo's personal darkie, under the name of Clarence Edmo. Sworn by Teton Sioux tribal law, according to the seal.

"Don't know much about Indians," Clevis admitted.

"Still got sovereignty. For now. This'll stand for anyone who isn't of a mind to tear it up and tell you they never saw it."

Clevis knew nothing would hold up before that kind of white man.

Edmo handed him a knitted cap with an Ottawa Senators logo. "Wear this, walk with your shoulders down, and for the love of God, man, if we get separated, head east as soon as you can. 89 goes out of Logan toward Bear Lake, but you'll want 30 out of Garden City."

Clevis took his new papers and his hat, shook Edmo's hand, and got into the back of the truck, preparing for the border crossing as a good darkie should.

※

At first Utah was an anticlimax. The militia at the border looked at Edmo, barely glanced at Clevis, and waved them on.

He stayed in the back, wondering how far Edmo would take him. Could he get Momma and Lindy out as the Indian's slaves? Estes Park was a long way from Edmo's home ground. Somehow it didn't seem likely.

They drove along the edge of the Wasatch-Cache National Forest, an upland expanse of hilly pines that walked along the taller mountains beyond. It was cold in the back, but Edmo had horse blankets amid the tools and bits of tack, and Clevis wrapped himself tight and day-dreamed of better, warmer times.

Despite Edmo's warnings about Utah, the state seemed

asleep. The tribal seal on Clevis's papers didn't appear to impress anyone at the checkpoints they reached, but he and Edmo kept getting waved along, making up miles it would have taken Clevis days and days to walk.

There wasn't trouble again until Sage Creek Junction, just a few miles from the Wyoming border. From there it would be a haul across the high, dry southwest corner of Wyoming, then on into Colorado. Assuming they made it out of Mormon country.

Sage Creek Junction was where he learned why Utah was so dangerous.

A news story over the wire. Datelined Portland, Oregon. Headline: "Famous Abolition Activist Goes Missing." Speculation that he was abducted or murdered by Red State security teams. The theory that he's slipped back over the border.

Accusations of journalistic irresponsibility fly: if Blackburn is back in slave territory, the media has practically told the Red States he's coming.

The Interamerican Reconciliation Commission, meeting in permanent session in Saskatoon under Russian and Canadian auspices, promises an investigation. The highest levels of government stir into action.

In the Blue States: "Where is Clevis Blackburn?"

In the Red States: "Who the hell cares about a troublesome darkie?"

But even slaves read the newspapers, some of them.

※

Flat as sin but more boring, Sage Creek Junction was tawny yellow almost as far as the eye could see, all the way to where the horizon was interrupted by foothills.

And between them and the horizon to the east was a string of what Clevis had first thought looked like lamp posts and could now see were rotting corpses on display, a tribute to and reminder of Utah justice.

As Edmo's pickup neared the few rustic wooden buildings that comprised the town, the old Indian slowed to the posted limit of only 20 mph. Clevis resisted the temptation to hide under the blankets and did his best to take in his surroundings with what he hoped was a vacant stare, the knitted cap low on his forehead. He remained with his back leaning against the right side of the truck bed, knees up beneath the blankets and his hands dangling between them.

Four heavy-set men with baseball caps over closely-cropped hair stepped into the road, forcing Sam Edmo to stop. The biggest of the four pushed his dirty green cap up a bit on his forehead. "Hey, Injun, that a runaway darkie you got in the back of your truck?"

Edmo leaned out of the window, one hand on the steering wheel, engine idling. "If he were a runaway, why would I be headin' east with him?"

"Yeah, why *are* you headin' east with him?" another man asked, punctuating his question with a massive wad of spit and phlegm in the dust between his feet and the pickup.

"Going to a pow-wow in the Ute Reservation in southern Colorado," the Indian said without blinking an eye. "Don't see any reason why I would have to do without him there."

Pow-wow. Clevis barely repressed a grimace, but Sam Edmo seemed to know what he was doing, because none of the white men blocking their truck made any sign of reacting to the silly fake-injun vocabulary.

"The Uintah Reservation is south," the first man said.

"No reason to come through here to get to Colorado."

"I'm Shoshone-Bannock from Fort Hall in Idaho." Edmo shrugged. "Gotta go through either Wyoming or Utah or both to get to the Ute Reservation."

A third man in black overalls pulled out a pocket watch and flipped it open. Something glittered in the bright fall sun, the light glancing off what looked like...a medallion.

"I don't know about you three, but m'first wife's a mean cook, and today's her turn at the stove." He glanced around, eyes not resting on Clevis, who watched half-lidded from beneath his knit cap. "Any of you see any reason to hold the Injun up any longer?"

The biggest one with the dirty green hat scratched his head for a moment and then pulled the brim down to just above his eyebrows again. "Nah." He stepped back and waved the pickup through. "Have a good pow-wow, red man."

After the rest of the men moved aside, the truck started forward again. It wasn't until Clevis took a deep breath that he realized he'd been holding it.

As they rolled past the baseball-capped farmers, the one in the black overalls examined his pocket watch again, allowing the sunlight to catch the gleaming surface just as Clevis came level with him.

A medallion with the image of his wife's face, glinting in the late afternoon sun. In the hands of a red-neck Mormon with more than one wife.

Who may just have saved their lives.

✺

Once they were waved through the checkpoint at the Wyoming border, a mere five minutes after they'd left the rotting corpses behind them, Edmo pulled off at the side of the road to take a leak, and Clevis joined him.

At least even here, in the Red States, a black man could piss at the side of the road same as a man of any other color.

"I hear they're lookin' harder for you now," Edmo said, shaking himself off and zipping up. "Made a call while you were in back, told 'em I won't be home for a while. My daughter said some damn liberal newspapers running stories about you slipping back into slave territory."

Just what he needed.

"Idiots."

"My thinking exactly." The Indian grinned. "At least

those folks back in Utah don't read liberal Blue State papers."

Clevis rebuttoned his jeans. "Except maybe one."

Edmo headed back for the car. "Ah, you saw that too."

"I saw that too."

"May be good for us, you know — Wrong-Way Blackburn got himself a following. Never know when that might come in handy."

"Like it did five minutes ago," Clevis murmured. Halfway to the rust-colored pickup, he stopped. "Go back to your daughter, Mr. Edmo. If it's getting more dangerous for me, I've got no business dragging anyone else into this."

Edmo gave him a long, thoughtful look. "I'd argue with you if I thought it'd do any good at all, Mr. Blackburn. But if there's any man in these United States who can find his own way, it's you." The old Indian took a deep breath. "I reckon if you think that's best, that's what I need to let you do."

They shook hands there, by the side of the road, and Clevis headed east and south, stepping into the long miles back to Colorado.

※

In the days that followed, Clevis met little that worried him. There were the ordinary kindnesses and cruelties of the road, rides given and threats offered and sometimes, rarely enough, food or a little cash.

Once or twice he thought he saw the copper flash of a certain familiar medallion, but a conspiracy of silence seemed to have settled over the Red States with respect to whatever was really happening in his life. To his wife.

She was *dead*.

He'd buried her himself.

What was he doing?

The mountains, the forests, the high-altitude farms and ranches and nearly-ghost towns and crumbling highway bridges gave him no useful answer at all. He was returning for Lindy. He knew that. If she'd passed away, word would have reached him. Hell, it might have been *news*.

He was not the last slave, after all, no matter what *The Economist* might call him. He was just a man. A father.

(A husband.)

Going to fetch his daughter home.

That thought sustained him past the questions and over the miles, across the southwest corner of Wyoming and, without any event whatsoever, into his native Colorado. All the hatred and violence of Idaho and Utah seemed to have melted into the studied indifference to darkies practiced by the entire American heartland.

Here, he was nothing more than mobile furniture. A tool with thumbs. A fixture that possessed the power of speech, when it was convenient for a white man to speak to him.

And he was going home.

So the miles wandered by beneath his feet, in the back of work trucks, in old cars filled with darkies willing to give a ride in exchange for news or rumors. In this manner, Clevis finally came back to Estes Park.

After crossing hundreds of miles without incident worse than some thrown beer bottles, Clevis found himself on Highway 63, walking among mountains whose names he'd known in his youth. The city of his birth sat in a sort of high-altitude bowl, surrounded on all sides by peaks already banded with snow, their arrayed ranks of sentinel pines silvered as if with age.

This was the country of his heart. Though he understood now what had been robbed from him as a child, they had never taken away the beauty in which he lived. The beauty had sustained him, the Heaven-high arch of the sky, the sweeping crags, the rolling plains in which the town nestled.

This was the country of his love, too, where he had courted Doreen in long walks through the tall grass, in a borrowed car driven carefully up the high meadows of Rocky Mountain National Park, by moonlight in the chill summers.

"What you doing, boy?"

Clevis startled out of his reverie to find himself staring at a cop. A familiar cop. A hundred yards ahead of him a cruiser idled on the gravel edge of the road, a Crown Victoria with enough chrome and lights to be its own sunrise if it were dark.

And this cop was Reggie Barnstone. White kid, his own age, used to run with the darkies on the weekends making trouble. Screwed the darkie women, too, confident no one would tell.

He had false papers. Edmo's papers. Barnstone would

know exactly who the hell Clevis was, if he bothered to think through what he saw and what he remembered.

"Walking into town, sir," Clevis mumbled, watching the road. There was no point in fighting Barnstone, even if Clevis had had the strength and training.

No darkie ever bought freedom on the flat of a fist.

Then the question he'd been dreading. "Don't I know you, boy?"

Clevis held his silence long enough to be respectful, not so long as to be sass. Though sass was always what a white man said it was. "Don't reckon so, sir. I'm sorry, sir."

Barnstone dug into his pocket, pulled out a copper medallion, began flipping it from one finger to the next in a lightly-closed fist. It was a coin trick he'd had when they were all kids. Clevis never did understand why it impressed the girls so much.

He knew that medallion. And he knew Reggie was clear on whose face was stamped upon it.

"You might be from around here, boy," Barnstone said. There was a careful edge in the cop's voice now, not the flat challenge of before.

Think, man, Clevis told himself. *He's offering you a way out. Otherwise he'd already be busting your head.* "Could be, sir," he said, his voice neutral as he could make it. Then, a chance on what was really going here. "A man's memory might change over time. His history might change over time. *Sir.*"

"Might. Might could change at that." Barnstone cleared his throat. The medallion flashed in the afternoon sun. "So...what kind of *trouble* would bring a man who'd long picked up his feet back here to our dusty little mountain paradise?"

"No trouble, sir." Quickly this time, step into the question. *Stay ahead of him.* "Just family. Not looking for nothing but a little old history. Then I'll be dust, sir."

"Dust." The medallion vanished. Into his fist, Clevis knew. Simple stage magic. "Dust is good, boy. Stay low."

Barnstone turned and walked back to his cruiser. Clevis shuffled about six paces behind, not wanting to overtake, not wanting to stand dumb as a signpost. When Barnstone got to the Ford, he tugged the door open, then turned to meet Clevis' eye.

"Be careful, Wrong-Way. More riding on this than you

know." The medallion flashed again, spinning in the air toward Clevis. He caught it as the cop slammed the door. The cruiser dropped into gear, then Barnstone pulled a 'u,' spraying Clevis with gravel and more dust.

He stood, the second medallion in his hand, convinced he should just go home right now.

What the hell was going on?

In the distance, there was the familiar chatter of helicopters.

Five miles from Lindy, and they're coming for me. Damn me for a punk-ass white kid.

His daughter was not going to finish growing up in this place. No matter what.

※

A flash of skin in the high mountain sun, a laugh, a herd of elk, a secret smile. A few moments as close to perfect as moments can get.

Then the two white kids who stumbled upon them. Or had they followed?

They made Clevis watch. Doreen had gone somewhere far away in her mind, but she still saw the way his hands clenched at his sides while one of them held him. She looked him straight in the eyes and gave a short shake of her head.

And the anger began to build.

But if there was one thing a slave learned in order to survive, it was how to channel anger.

The helicopters in the sky meant he couldn't go straight to Momma, pick them up, and head west. As if he ever could have done that.

The safest place until he figured out what to do would be where there were a lot of darkies - below-stairs at one of the many resorts nestled up into the mountains rising up on all sides of Estes Park.

Clevis pulled the knitted cap lower on his forehead and turned down Highway 34 where it curled around the north side of Lake Estes on the edge of town. The help at the first lakeside lodge turned him away with a shrug, but at the second, they let him in with hardly a word.

A young woman with high cheekbones and skin so black she looked African handed him a uniform in shades of green and brown. "The whiteys pay the least amount of attention to the darkies on garbage duty. Jim's at the end of the hall — he'll tell you what to do."

"Thanks kindly, ma'am."

A slight smile lightened her stern features. "It's an honor helping the famous Wrong-Way. None of us want those choppers to find what they're looking for."

Clevis was slowly being overcome by a sense of awe — where had all these people come from who knew him, knew about him, were willing to help him? How had be become a figure for people to rally behind?

Here in Estes Park, the medallion with the face of a dead woman was nearly as common as coin, and soon Clevis knew he would have a small army at his back when his preparations had been completed for smuggling Lindy and Momma away. Of course, only a few of them could vacate their posts at the Lakeshore Inn at a time, and then only with a good excuse, but slaves nowadays had a freedom of movement unimaginable a hundred years ago.

Ah yes, so much to be thankful for.

After a week collecting garbage, Clevis was nearly ready to make his move. The presence of the helicopters had diminished, and he and those who carried medallions had scouted his mother's house, counting the unmarked cop cars and noting when shifts changed and the numbers were lowest. From a distance, Clevis watched as his daughter left for school in the morning, watched and forced himself not to go to her, even though his arms ached to enfold her thin body, feel her fidgety child's warmth again.

During the long, hushed discussions in the slave quarters, they had decided to get Lindy and Momma away separately. Clarice, the stately young black woman he'd met the first day, had visited Momma already and warned her; while Clarice was getting Lindy away after school, Jim would pick Momma up to "go shopping."

Clevis was emptying garbage cans into the big bins near the service driveway when he saw a rust-colored pickup with Idaho plates pull into the parking lot of the lodge.

He couldn't help himself — he stared.

"Hey, darkie, what you doin' standin' around — you need more work?"

Clevis dragged his attention away from the familiar truck and pulled down the brim of his cap with a deferential nod to the white supervisor. "Nossir. Sorry, sir."

The supervisor looked at him more closely. "What's your name, boy?"

"Leon, sir." There were three Leons at Lakeshore, making it one of the least suspicious names here in the lodge.

"Get back to work, Leon, or you'll end up thinking garbage is the sweetest thing you ever smelled."

"Yessir."

After the supervisor left, Clevis began to go from room to room emptying trash cans and searching for Sam Edmo. He found the old Indian in a small ground-floor room without a view.

"Having a nice vacation, sir?" Clevis asked.

"Ain't a vacation, really," Edmo said. "Need to pick something up."

"Here in Estes Park?"

"Down by the fairgrounds. Then I'll be heading back to Fort Hall in Idaho."

They exchanged a long look, and Clevis nodded. "Good luck, sir, and have a good trip back."

If Sam Edmo could get Lindy and Momma out fast, their

biggest worry would be solved.

※

The Colored school was in the southeastern part of town, away from the desirable tourist property in the foothills and around the lake. It consisted of simple prefab units, worn and discolored with age, discards from some temporary government project but still good enough for the children of the Colored labor pool. The buildings should have been replaced when Clevis was a child, and now here was Lindy going to the same school.

The air was clear and crisp, a perfect fall day, sunny with a hint of cold. Clevis watched the door from the comparative safety of the bushes along the edge of the overgrown playground, feeling his heart wrench, knowing he would soon see his beautiful young daughter again — and this time, he would hold her and talk to her.

And put her in danger.

No, he couldn't think about that. He had to get her away, and they had done everything they could to keep her safe.

The first children were coming out of the door and Clarice had appeared to pick up Lindy, when the sound of helicopters blossomed in the sky again as three cop cars appeared around the corner, squealing to a halt in front of the makeshift school building.

How had they known?

The children who had already left the building were cowering in a small huddle, and those just leaving froze in the doorway.

Lindy.

Car doors opened, uniformed officers appeared, and there was a staccato of slamming doors punctuating the more continuous rhythm of the choppers above.

Lindy stood on the wooden plank steps of the prefab building, staring at the cops with her classmates.

Don't go to her, Clarice!

Two of the policemen scanned the faces of the kids and then moved towards the stairs while the other four stayed near their cars. They were heading straight for his daughter — they hadn't known, they were just trying to draw him out, use the most effective weapon they had on him.

They reached the stairs and one of the cops took Lindy's bony shoulder in his meaty paw and forced her down the stairs.

It wouldn't help her at all if he came out of hiding, but how could he not?

Lindy cried out, tears starting in her eyes, and before Clevis knew it, he was dashing across the playground with the scream of rage that had been choked in his throat since that day in the high mountain meadow, that day of sunlight and pain.

"Daddy!"

Handguns came out of holsters and rifles were lifted to shoulders, but Clevis couldn't bother with that now. Voices called out for him to stop, to give himself up, voices far away from the world of his daughter's tears and the white man with his hand on her, far away from the rage that consumed him.

As he neared the school building, the other children scattered. The cop who had been man-handling Lindy let her go to reach for his own gun, but he had barely gotten it out of his holster when Clevis tackled him.

"Run, Lindy!"

And then Clevis was rolling on the ground with the

thick-set cop, slamming his fist into his face, arm-wrestling him for the gun. He could hear more shouted commands, feel hands on his arms and shoulders, trying to pull him off, all somewhere outside of the haze of anger that had him in its grip. And then he had the gun, and the cop beneath him was screaming, bleeding, while Clevis pounded him with the butt, and the rest of the cops pulled him off their buddy.

His arms were yanked behind him and handcuffs clamped on. Panting, Clevis looked around.

No sign of Lindy or Clarice.

Through the fog that was slowly leaving him, Clevis felt a fierce joy, a hope he couldn't contain: his daughter had gotten away. Edmo would see to it she made it to a safe house and to freedom, he knew it.

And then they threw him to the ground and started kicking him.

※

He woke up in a cold cell, hard pallet between gray walls, every inch of his body aching. Breathing was a stabbing pain, and he wondered how many of his ribs were broken.

A key rattled in the lock and he turned his head to the

door of his cage.

"Doc here to see you," said the burly guard. "Though I don't see why, since you're hangin' sure enough after what you did to Frank."

"Protocol needs to be followed," came a soft voice behind him. "And we can't make a martyr of this particular slave or we'll have more trouble on our hands than we can manage."

She stepped out from behind the guard and into his cell — and Clevis's breathing suddenly became even more difficult.

It was a white woman with the face of his wife.

"Can you take off your shirt, Mr. Blackburn, or should the guard assist you?"

Clevis was still staring, incapable of replying. Green eyes, high cheekbones, a long nose with a patrician bump on the bridge. Doreen's nose had been wider, but otherwise it was the same face except for the color of the skin.

The guard came to his bunk and yanked him up. Clevis screamed with the pain.

"Answer the doc when she speaks to you, Darkie." His breath was garlic and old tobacco.

"That was unnecessary, Mr. Gibbon," the white ghost said, her voice cool and professional. "We have to see that this man survives until his trial."

"Darkies don't need no trial," Gibbon muttered.

The doctor grimaced. "Unfortunately, this one does."

Clevis finally found his voice. "I can get my shirt off myself."

The doctor moved to his side with her black bag and snapped it open. "Good."

As he began to unbutton the shirt, Clevis thought he had promised too much. Every movement sent shooting pain through his chest, and he could only peel the shirt slowly from his aching body. In the bloody patches, the fabric stuck to his skin.

The doctor swabbed the wounds so she could pull the material away, and he was able to see her name tag. Varin. The name of the family that had owned Doreen's parents before turning their slaves over to the Estes Park labor pool because they were more trouble than they were worth.

Doctor Varin began probing his chest with cool, capable hands, while Gibbon looked on, sullenly massive.

"Wince and cry out," she murmured near his ear.

Clevis was so surprised, all he could do was suck in his breath.

"I never knew I had a sister until she was dead," the doctor added in a whisper. "I don't want the father of my only niece to die the same way."

With those words, she prodded one of his aching ribs where the skin was mottled with bruises. It was easy enough to follow her directions; other than his scream when Gibbon yanked him up, Clevis has been holding his pain in.

"Again."

He gave a another yelp, and another, as she prodded down his chest and around his back.

Dr. Varin stepped back and folded her arms in front of her chest, looking at him critically. "As far as I can determine from a superficial examination, at least half his ribs are broken. We have to transfer him to the hospital facilities in Longmont — it's a wonder a lung wasn't punctured."

Gibbon grumbled, sounding as if he was about to spit out a chaw on the spot. "Good riddance, I say."

She shook her head and pulled out a cell phone. "You

heard what the chief said. There can't be any suspicion attached to the authorities where Clevis Blackburn is concerned. He may just be a runaway slave, but he's more famous than either one of us."

The guard snorted. "No justice in the world."

"Hello, Officer?" Dr. Varin said into her cell. "We need to arrange for transportation of the prisoner to a hospital." She paused, listening to someone Clevis couldn't hear. "Yes, that would be fine. Goodbye."

She flicked the phone closed. "A police car will be here in about fifteen minutes. Do you think you can walk, Mr. Blackburn?"

Clevis nodded mutely, and Gibbon came forward with handcuffs. Standing was a shaky business, but not as painful as breathing. The guard snapped the cuffs on his wrists and together they shuffled out of the cell and down a short corridor with cells on either side; Estes Park was too small for a large jail facility, and besides, that wouldn't be good for tourism. Clevis was dying to ask about Lindy, but he couldn't say anything with Gibbon gripping his elbow.

Another guard opened a further cage door, and then they

were in the entrance hall of the small jail where the windows were larger and autumn sunlight streamed in like a gift that Clevis had to squint to accept. They pushed him down on a hard wooden bench. It was an effort just to keep sitting up straight and breathing regularly.

"Any news of the runaways?" Dr. Varin asked the guards while they were waiting for the police escort. Clevis could have gone down on his knees in thanks.

The second guard shook his head. "Best forces are on it, though. Won't be long before we get them back."

Drive far and fast, Sam Edmo, and God keep you safe.

Then there was the sound of a car pulling up in front of the building, and the guards were yanking him to his feet again and taking him outside, Dr. Varin leading the way.

Reggie Barnstone got out of the cruiser parked at the curb, sunglasses hiding his blue eyes. He folded his arms in front of his chest and leaned against the vehicle, looking every bit the mean sonovabitch.

"The prisoner needs to be taken to the hospital in Longmont," Dr. Varin said.

Reggie nodded, his expression unchanging, and opened

the rear door. The guards hustled him in none too gently. The car door slammed behind him and Reggie got in the front seat and started the car.

"Forget about the dust, Wrong-Way," Reggie said as they turned east on Highway 36. "You're here for good now."

Clevis's hopes sank. For one wild moment when he saw Reggie emerge from the cruiser, he'd thought, maybe, somehow they'd arranged for him to escape and get back to Lindy.

"What's left of these United States needs the direction someone like Wrong-Way Blackburn will take it," Reggie continued. "I think you'll find something there on the back seat next to you."

Clevis looked down. Tucked into the crack where the seat cushion met the back was an unmarked envelop. He picked it up with his manacled hands and tore it open. Inside was a key.

Reggie glanced at him in the rearview mirror. "Prisoners can be a violent lot. Not all of them get where they're supposed to go."

The key fit the lock on the handcuffs perfectly, and they opened with a small *click*.

Clevis grinned. "How badly you need to be beaten up, old buddy?"

His one-time pal grimaced. "I knew there was a reason I shouldn't've volunteered for this job. Maybe we should just roll the car."

"Might be better. Don't know how much people will believe with half my ribs cracked."

Reggie nodded. "I'll run us into a tree. By the way, got a message for you from some old Injun. Says you should visit Fort Hall sometime."

Clevis's heart opened up like the manacles he'd just taken off his wrists. "I think maybe I'll do that."

END

The Canadian Who Came Almost All the Way Home From the Stars

Kelly MacInnes was pretty, prettier than I had expected. She had that sort of husky blonde beauty I associated with the upper Midwest. Or in her case, the Canadian prairie.

Together we stared out across Emerald Lake, one of those small mountain lakes jeweling western North America, framed by a vista of Douglas firs, longleaf pines and granite peaks clawing their way into the echoing summer sky. Midway out on the lake, the water gathered into a visible depression, as if a huge weight had settled on it. The dimple was about forty feet in diameter and ten feet deep, perfectly flat at the bottom, with steeply-angled sides like a giant inverted bottle cap. It had appeared five days after Nick MacInnes had mysteriously called home three months ago — years after he was presumed dead.

At which point Nick's widow had promptly dropped everything and come here to Yoho National Park in darkest British Columbia.

"It looks unnatural." It was a dumb thing to say, but I didn't have much to offer. I was an intruder after all, a U.S. agent come to investigate phone call and dimple — and Mrs. MacInnes.

"It *is* unnatural," she replied. "A couple of weeks after it appeared, every fish in the lake had beached or moved downstream."

I could imagine the rot. Such a stench seemed impossible in this mountain paradise. The air had the sharp tang of snow on pines, the flinty odor of wet rock, the absolute purity of the Canadian Rockies.

But there was a lot that was impossible going on here. I had seen the satellite tracking reports — NORAD, NASA, ESA, even some Chinese data. The dimple had appeared, fish had died — *something* had happened — but there was no evidence of re-entry, no evidence of any precipitating event whatsoever. Only the hole in the lake in front of me.

And a phone call that couldn't have happened, from a dead man lost in interstellar space.

"You say your husband told you to come here." They'd all asked her the questions before: the RCMP, the Special Branch, the FBI, several UN High Commissions. Kelly MacInnes had met her husband in college where they both studied astrophysics, but her name had never been on any of his papers or patents. They asked her the questions anyway.

And now it was my turn, on behalf of the NSA. We still didn't know what had happened out there in that lake, but we wanted to make sure no one else knew either. The first step had been to clear out the park — except for Kelly MacInnes. My job wasn't as much to drag information out of her as it was to make sure it didn't get to anyone else first if she was moved to start talking.

She stared out at the hole in the water, the unfilled grave of her absent husband. "He's not dead."

I nodded. "I've read the transcripts — it's clear to me you believe that." *Or at least you claim you do.* "But, Mrs. MacInnes, there is no evidence your husband survived his rather spectacular departure from earth six years ago."

She hugged her plaid flannel jacket closer, her gaze drifting up to the sky. Despite the sun, the air was crisp. "The trip was supposed to take less than a week. Then six years after he left, he called and told me to meet him here. Just after 2:30 am on April 17th, the center of the lake collapsed into that hole. That's what I know, Mr. Diedrich."

I followed her stare toward the summer sky. Somewhere behind that perfect blue shell was an explanation for what happened to Nicholas MacInnes.

Too bad the sky wasn't talking today.

Barnard's star is slightly less than six light years from Sol. A red dwarf, it is interesting only for its convenient position in the interstellar neighborhood and the fact that it is moving noticeably faster than any of our other stellar neighbors.

Until Nick MacInnes decided to go there six years ago.

Four years prior to his launch, he'd published a paper in the *Canadian Journal of Aerospace Engineering and Technology Applications*, "Proposal for a Cost-Effective Method of Superluminal Travel." *CJAETA* was about one step above vanity publishing, and the article was soon well on its way to the dustbin of history.

Recently, I had seen to it that all copies of Volume XXXVI, Issue 9, had been destroyed, along with computer files, Web sites, mirror sites, tape backups, printer plates, CD-ROMS, library microfiche archives and everything else we could think of. Because one fine spring day, Nick MacInnes, sometime mobile communications billionaire, made a space shot from a privately-built and previously unknown launch site on the prairie east of Calgary, found his way into orbit on top of surplus Russian missile hardware, and did something that crashed a significant portion of the world's electronic infrastructure. At which point, he disappeared in a rainbow-colored flash visible across an entire hemisphere of the planet.

It soon became known that he was carrying four surplus Russian M-2 nuclear warheads. "For the bomb-pumped lasers," the Ph.D.s assisting MacInnes said, as if the rest of the world were worrying excessively over trivialities.

※

When I returned to Emerald Lake three months later to check on Kelly MacInnes and security at the park, the Canadian Air Force and NASA were back. The CAF had flown a Lockheed Orion P-3C AIP over the lake back in late April and through most of May. Now, in October, NASA and the Canadian Space Agency had stuck some added instrumentation on it. They gave up on towed sonar after losing two rigs in the trees along the shoreline. Variously operated satellites had performed various kinds of imaging and discovered a significant gravitational anomaly at the bottom of Emerald Lake. Or maybe they hadn't. The dimple in the lake surface was caused by the stress of the anomaly. Or maybe not.

There wasn't a ferrous body in the lake, but a significant masscon rested on the bottom, absorbing radar and creating weird thermal gradients. Wild theories were thrown around concerning polymerization of water, stress on molecular bonds, microscopic black holes, time singularities and so on. There was some hard data about a heat rise in the center of the dimple, a heat rise that declined in temperature during the first three weeks of observation before leveling out about nine degrees centigrade above historical ambient surface temperature. Curiously, remote sensing indicated ice at the bottom of the lake in the area of the dimple. Cameras and instrument packages sent down didn't add much to the picture — the masscon was big, it was inert, and it distorted the lake's temperature profile.

But then the search for additional meaningful data was complicated by the one incontrovertible thing discovered besides the heat rise: radioactive contamination. Everyone working at the lake was being exposed to radionuclides equivalent to three hundred rem a year, sixty times the permitted exposure level for workers in the United States. Well into cancer-causing territory, especially leukemia, but not enough to give you an immediate case of the pink pukes or make your hair fall out.

When I heard, I sought out the CSA project manager in charge of the current phase of the investigation, Ray Vittori. I was no physicist, but I'd been a technology spook for years. This stank. "How in holy hell could you not have noticed this before?"

Vittori shook his head. "It wasn't here before, Diedrich. Simple."

I crossed my arms. Behind me, I thought I could feel Kelly MacInnes smile, but I didn't bother to turn around to see if I was right. She mistrusted government institutions, including her own, but Americans she loathed.

As it was, we couldn't justify trucking the required diving equipment, minisubs, and underwater instrumentation high into the Canadian Rockies to find out more about the dimple. So much data had already been collected that it would take years to analyze it in the first place. And the anomaly didn't seem to be going anywhere anytime soon. The radiation levels just complicated whatever case I might have made for increased allocation of intelligence assets.

The Orion went back to hunting subs in the Maritime Provinces. The think tanks went back to thinking somewhere else. Some cameras and sensors remained, wired in around the lakeshore, shooting telemetry back to my agency in Maryland. Other than that, only the satellites still provided us with information, along with the occasional research team willing to sign their souls away in indemnity clauses. A barebones contingent continued to secure the perimeters of the park, all volunteer agents at exorbitant pay for assurances that they wouldn't seek damages if they ever showed signs of sickness which could be attributed to radiation.

By the time the first snow fell, I was left alone to observe the astonishing natural beauty of Yoho National Park and the equally attractive Mrs. Kelly MacInnes. Just me, after all the attention and the hardware went away, with a dosimeter, a sixteen-foot bass boat, and lots of time.

※

We ate corned beef hash and canned peaches in the echoing stillness of the lodge's dining hall. The worst of winter was past, but it was damned cold anyway, and we wore down jackets everywhere — and extra layers when we dared to go outside.

"At least he picked a National Park," I said, looking around the empty lodge. My visits to Emerald Lake had been getting longer and longer over the winter. The agency kept me largely free, since it was hard to get anyone else to come up here with the threat of contamination. Not to mention the godawful remoteness.

And then there was Kelly. Nick knew what he was about, choosing this woman with the loyalty of a lioness. Though at times I rather imagined it was she who had done the choosing.

She smiled. "Quiet place, facilities nearby, eh, Mr. Diedrich?"

"I was thinking more in terms of access control. Difficult to secure and patrol private land."

Her big laugh rang out louder than was natural in the empty spaces of the lodge. "Do you see anyone trying to violate your vaunted security in this godforsaken place?"

I grimaced. A psychiatrist would probably have a field day with me — NSA spook falls for married woman who laughs at him.

But what a magnificent laugh it was.

I lowered my forkful of peach. "Why are *you* still here in this godforsaken place?" Kelly had plenty of money — Nick's misadventures in orbit had barely depleted his fortunes, even after the staggering fines assessed against his estate for sundry air traffic and orbital protocol violations. She could have checked on the dimple then headed for Tahiti.

She cocked her head. "I could ask you the same question, with more justification. I'm waiting for my husband, making sure you lot don't muck up his chances of returning. Keeping my eye on the dimple. What are *you* waiting for, Mr. Diedrich? Why do you keep coming back?"

I couldn't give her a true answer, not one that she would accept.

※

The melting of the snow was like a revelation.

Patches of green appeared in the unremitting white of the landscape just as the first anniversary of Nick MacInnes's telephone call from the stars approached.

In celebration of one or the other, Kelly and I hiked out to the lake to inspect the dimple. All winter long, it hadn't frozen over, despite the blankets of snow on all sides, despite the fact that other lakes in the region were solid sheets of ice.

The dimple still appeared much as it had the first day I had seen it, even with the snow on the north side of the lake — wide, unnatural, a mystery to be solved.

And the key stood next to me.

"In some ways I'm waiting for the same thing as you, you know," I said finally.

She was silent for a long time. I knew she understood me

— during the time we had spent together over the last winter, we had developed that odd pattern of shortcuts and silences that many married couples use to communicate. I just barely remembered it from my own failed marriage.

She nodded out at the dimple. "You were born in the United States?"

Non sequitur. We had advanced to those as well. But I still didn't know where she was going with this. "Yes."

"You've been on the winning team all your life. You don't have a clue what it's like to be Canadian, having the world's biggest brother next door." A hare hopped into our line of vision. I watched it make tracks in the snow left in the sun's shadow.

"The United States," Kelly continued, not looking at me. "The 'we did it first' country. You build the space shuttle, we build a robot arm. Canada makes another contribution to progress."

She seemed to expect a serious answer. I didn't give it to her.

"And now your government keeps sending you here to babysit me. Because the hard men with the bright lights didn't learn anything."

"No one is forcing me."

She gave me a look that asked me who I thought I was kidding, one eyebrow raised and her wide lips somewhere close to a smile. "No, but I know why you're here. You hate it, the whole world hates it, but especially you Yanks. You hate that a Canadian went to the stars first, without you."

She was partly right.

But only partly.

※

Kelly was a hard nut to crack, laughter or no laughter. It wasn't until we'd been alone together regularly for almost a year before she started calling me by my first name.

Even though I had been waiting for it for what seemed forever, I almost didn't notice. We were out on the lake in the park's Ranger Cherokee to take some measurements of our own of the surface temperature near the dimple, cross checking the instruments. My Geiger counter kept acting up — the third one the agency had sent me — but there was nothing wrong with our old-fashioned thermometers.

I had no interest in taking the boat into the middle. The

drop to the flat surface of the dimple was about ten feet and looked vaguely like a ring of waterfalls.

"I'm keeping at least five boat lengths away," I said. "We'll circle."

Kelly trailed the thermometer on a length of fishing line. "Fine with me, Bruce."

I was so busy navigating the rim of the dimple, the fact that she had called me "Bruce" didn't immediately register. When it did, it was like a kick to the gut, and I jerked the tiller towards the edge.

I corrected immediately and Kelly looked up. "Temperature holding steady here. What about you?"

"I'm fine."

The pines whistled with the mountain wind; even in July, it was chilly up here. As I drove the boat, I watched a hawk work the thermals off toward the granite massif that sheltered the headwaters of the Kicking Horse River. There was something seriously wrong with me if Kelly's use of my first name felt as intimate as a kiss.

It was about time I called my boss, Marge Williams, and returned to Maryland again for a while.

Somehow, I didn't have much success fleeing Emerald Lake. The next time I came back, I came back for good. The ostensible excuse was Marge's gentle insistence — the government still wanted whatever information Kelly MacInnes could provide badly enough to make it a permanent assignment. The potential value of what Nick had done, even with its fatal flaws, outweighed any cost of my time and effort.

But the real reason was Kelly. NSA couldn't force me, given the radiation risk — and they didn't have to.

I returned in October. To my surprise, she was waiting at the park landing zone as the helicopter came in.

"What took you so long!" she shouted out over the whirring of the blades as I hopped down from the cabin. "We've had no less than seven dimple-fans succeed in breaching security since you left."

"Seven! Guess I better get back on the job." Of course I had already been informed about the handful of trespassers who weren't bright enough to be scared off by radioactive fallout — Marge had used them as a further argument to get me to return. For the good of the project, of course. And

Kelly's safety. That and a huge bonus I could put aside to finance my medical bills if I ended up with cancer in a decade or two.

It all seemed worth it with Kelly glad to see me. Perhaps it was just the basic human need for companionship, but I was happy to delude myself into thinking it was more.

※

By our third year at Emerald Lake, it began to appear that the world had forgotten us. Over the winter, attempts to breach park security had dwindled to nothing, and even with the arrival of spring and the second anniversary of the appearance of the dimple, there had been less than half-a-dozen. Of course, I still spoke with headquarters nearly every week. We also had occasional contact with maintenance personnel and an RCMP trooper by the name of Sergeant Perry who actually came by on horseback when the weather was good and sometimes brought us old newspapers. I went back to Maryland regularly for my quarterly mission reviews and radiation assessments, and we were connected with the outside world through the Internet, but for the most part we were alone.

Me, Kelly, and the dimple.

She looked at that damn dimple every day as if Nick MacInnes was going to come walking out of it and embrace her. I just looked at it.

And so we hadn't become lovers. To me she was a widow, but Kelly thought of herself as a wife.

An extremely loyal wife.

We got along well enough, had even become friends of sorts. That is if you disregarded the fact that I dreamed about the scent of her every night.

It was a warm day in late August when I finally asked the question. "So, why are we still here?"

Kelly and I sat in front of the lodge on a little pebbled strip of land too modest to call a beach. The dimple punctuated the lake in front of us, and the mountains loomed high in the sky around it. For a change it was warm enough that I didn't have to wear a jacket.

"Why are *you* still here?"

I shrugged. "You're my job." You and Nick, I thought,

but I tried to say his name as little as possible. "According to my boss, they don't have anything else for me."

She placed her left hand on my right forearm, a rare moment of physical contact between us. "Oh, surely there's more for you to do than wait by a lake. You Americans, you always have some mess to go fix. Or make."

I didn't move a muscle, afraid to dislodge her touch. "I wouldn't have to be here all the time just to oversee the security of the site. Your husband achieved something no one ever did before him, and there are a lot of people who want to know what he didn't tell us." *What you're not telling us.* "Marge sent me here to find out why you're still keeping such a sharp eye on the dimple."

Kelly smiled, one eyebrow arched. "Marge?"

"Sure. Not everyone is as afraid of first names as you are."

She moved her hand away. Me and my big mouth. My arm still tingled where her fingers had been.

"Actually," she said, "I'm waiting for another message from him."

I couldn't help laughing. "Another phone call?"

She grinned. "No, no. Nick promised to set a sign in the heavens."

Despite her grin, I had the strange feeling that she was serious.

※

After the snows melted the next spring, Kelly started bugging me to go into the center of the dimple with her, a squint of worry around her eyes. The thing had never frozen over, even as the ice crusted around the edges. A heavy snow could cover it for a day or so, before the snow blanket sagged into the warm water beneath. The dimple was there like a great blind eye in the water, staring at the sky, trapping us in its unseeing gaze.

I studied the strange phenomenon which had become such an everyday part of life. "How do you propose we get back out if we go down in there?"

Kelly gazed at me speculatively. "How good a swimmer are you, Bruce?"

I shook my head. "No, no way."

She gave me her wide smile. I could almost believe I had imagined the worry — but only almost. "If we had a long enough rope with us, you could belay the boat back for sure. You're strong. I bet you're a good swimmer."

"I was all-New England in prep school," I admitted. "But I'm still not going to do it."

"Why not?"

Oh, Christ, Kelly. "One, I don't want to drown in those damned waterfalls. Two, I don't want to put my body near that thermal gradient without a boat between me and it. The overflight data suggested ice layers down there, at the reverse end of the heat rise. That's why we have cameras and instrument packages."

"Sometimes there's nothing like a first-hand look."

"No."

"You're already exposing yourself to constant radiation," she pointed out, flirting and pleading at the same time. I hadn't thought her capable of either. "Why not a simple masscon?"

This time I said it out loud. "Christ, Kelly."

She let loose a lovely peal of laughter and took my elbow. "Besides, it's not like you have anything else to do this summer."

When Kelly realized I wasn't going to get into that water for her anytime soon, she decided we needed to build a "dimple observatory." We spent several days hauling lumber from the park's maintenance shed to a beautiful old rock maple right up by the water with just the right spread of branches. Kelly's big laugh echoed between the trees and the mountains more often than I had ever heard it as we messed with ropes and nails, building our tree fort.

I had thought I was lost in love before, but I hadn't known how charming, how fun she could be.

Our Mountie showed up while we were up there hammering away. He regarded us seriously for a moment from his big bay mare, like a critical parent.

Kelly took the nail out of her mouth and called down to him. "Come on, Sergeant Perry. Don't you want to work on a tree fort again?"

He cracked a smile and gave us a few hours of his time. I finally thanked him for his help when I noticed him watching his dosimeter more carefully than he was watching the hammer in his hand.

One night Kelly and I were grilling hot dogs over a campfire next to our "observatory" when she gave me *that look* again. "Bruce, won't you at least take me out to the surface of the dimple? I want to see it for myself."

"Christ, Kelly." I pulled my dog out of the fire and tried to brush off some of the burned spots. What the hell. I'd already signed up for cancer for her sake, had been throwing away redlined dosimeters for a while. "Sure."

She tackled me with a squeal that made it all worthwhile. I hoped.

※

"How deep can you dive?"

I looked up from the gear I was stowing in the Ranger Cherokee. I hadn't done any diving in years. "Now wait a minute — "

"If you're going into the water anyway, you could also see if you could get down to the masscon."

I straightened, shaking my head. "The anomaly is in thirty meters of water. I don't think I can hold my breath more than ninety seconds. That's not enough."

"So we tie a fifteen meter rope to your ankle, drop you

over with something heavy to take you down fast, and you push a pole down the rest of the way."

I laughed. "And do what? Tap?"

She smiled her real smile. "You come back up, tell me what you saw, what it felt like. What's down there."

"You were planning on asking me this all along, weren't you?"

Her smile took on a guilty cast. "Well, yes."

I sighed. How much did it matter now? There wasn't much I could do to compete with her rich, dead, genius husband. At least I could do this for her.

I wired the butt of an ancient oak post to the end of a twenty-foot aspen pole, then made a wrist loop at the other end of the pole out of an old bootlace. I would jump head first out of the bass boat clutching an old wheel rim to weigh me down, and follow the pole toward the bottom. But first I smeared my body with a mixture of Vaseline and mud — we didn't have enough of the petroleum jelly around the lodge to use it straight up, but I was worried about the cold.

"We're nuts," I said. Kelly drove the boat straight for the dimple. Our long line trailed behind us toward the nearest shore, some two hundred feet distant, ready for my belaying act.

Kelly looked happier than she had since I first met her. "Nick's down there."

"I'm not knocking on any doors." I already had mud in some very uncomfortable places.

Her smile was like the sunrise. "Just see what you see."

What I saw was what Nick MacInnes had seen in her. What I wondered was what she had seen in him: the record suggested he had been a monomaniacal nutcase who happened to have gotten it right.

The Ranger Cherokee slid down into the dimple, and my stomach did a sharp flop — the world's shortest log flume ride. Kelly cut the trolling motor, and the boat circled loosely in the base of the dimple, a forty-foot wide bowl. The ten foot walls of water around us were incredibly disconcerting, a violation of every sense and sensibility. It didn't help that our trailing line strained *upward*, vanishing to those angled waterfalls.

We tipped the stripped aspen pole overboard. The oak block pulled it straight down until it was stopped by the bootlace loop I'd slipped over a cleat, rocking our little boat. I stared down at the rippling black water, beneath which lay the masscon.

"Don't think too hard," said Kelly. "You won't do it."

I checked the knot of the life line on my ankle. I was only doing it for her, and she was doing it for her husband — she was right, I'd better not think too hard. "Count to thirty, then start pulling up, as fast as you can." I slipped my hand through the loop on the gunwale cleat, pulled the pole free with the tether around my wrist, and fell in head first, clutching the wheel rim to my chest.

The water wasn't any colder than I expected, but it pushed up my nose in a way that seemed stronger, sharper than reasonable. Venting a little air from my lips, I released the wheel rim; I was getting enough downward pull from the weighted aspen pole.

My ears throbbed with mild pain. The breathing panic started, but I ignored it, letting the pole drag me down past the visible light.

The water got cooler as I sank. I wondered how deep I was, wondered if Kelly had tossed my line over, sending me off to meet her husband. My ankle jerked up short, and I almost lost my grip on the pole, but the bootlace loop around my wrist held.

I bobbed head down for a moment, the pole pulling me down, the rope holding me back. I worked my hands to get a firmer grip on the pole. With my eyes open, there was a vague greenish quality to the darkness. The water pressure on my body was like a giant fist slowly closing.

That was when I realized my fingers were cold, way too cold. I brought my free hand up in front of my face, but there wasn't enough light to see it. I touched my fingers to my lips — ice scum. I knew what the reports had said, but still ... water froze from the *top*, not the *bottom*.

Then the pole jumped in my hands. The downward pull was gone, the pole floating slowly upward. What had happened to the weight? My chest tightened with anoxia and fear. The water felt much colder. Where the hell was Kelly? I tried to turn my body, but with the pole in the way, I started to get trapped in the rope.

My ankle jerked.

Kelly.

Thank God.

I held the pole while she tugged the rope from somewhere inside the blue sky far above. I followed my heart toward the bright air.

※

Kelly wrapped me in two blankets when I rolled into the boat, and I shivered in their scratchy depths. I didn't have the strength to swim to shore yet.

She examined the aspen pole. "Looks like it snapped off."

I shook my head. Now that I wasn't panicking, it was easier to figure out what might have happened to the pole. "No applied pressure — I would have felt that."

Kelly pointed the broken end toward me. The end looked more like it had been blown off. Would my hand have done the same, under the pressure of the rapidly expanding ice?

Kelly came to the same conclusion at about the same time. "Cold," she said, her voice strangely satisfied. "The aspen shattered from the cold."

"What's so great about cold?" The cold could have killed me. I was feeling groggy from the dive, chilled in the half-hearted sun of the Canadian Rockies.

Her smile flashed. "Very slow entropic progression, that's what's so great about cold."

Very slow entropic progression. I'd never heard her talk like that before.

※

The following winter, we were enjoying a comfortable afternoon in front of the lodge fireplace when we heard shots. We looked at each other in shock for a moment before we jumped up, pulled on our Gore-tex snowpants and parkas, and headed out for the snowmobile.

Less than a mile from the lodge, we found Sergeant Perry's body in the snow, his skis sticking up at an odd angle, his blood spattering the pristine white of the landscape.

Kelly stifled a sob, then bent to close his eyes. I had to stop myself from reaching to comfort her, so I scanned the woods for signs of movement instead. Nothing.

I called Maryland. There wasn't much point in seeking cover — if the shooter was still out there, we were in their sights.

"Perhaps it was a hunting accident?" Marge said, her

voice perplexed over the static-filled connection.

"A hunting accident?" Islamists, Chinese, environmentalists — I could think of a lot more likely explanations than that. "Marge, no one should be able get past our security for there to *be* a hunting accident. You need to initiate an outside investigation."

Kelly knelt in the snow next to the body, tears streaming down her face. We hadn't known the Mountie well, but he had been one of the few people we'd had any contact with in the last four-plus years.

On the other end of the line, Marge sighed. "You're right, this needs to be looked into. I'll take care of it, Bruce."

"Thanks."

An NSA helicopter flew in to collect the body and take Perry back to wherever he had come from. Kelly and I watched it wing away again, and to my surprise, her arm slid around my waist.

I had the odd thought that I wished I could die right then, standing in the snow like one half of a couple with Kelly MacInnes.

※

The dimple was definitely changing. During the summer following Sergeant Perry's mysterious death — which the NSA had failed to clear up — it had grown visibly wider and shallower. Even with our crude measurements, the heat rise was becoming noticeably greater. Radiation levels remained stable however — the dosimeters and my Geiger counter were consistent.

I suggested calling in surveillance aircraft from the agency once more, but Kelly would have none of it. "What good are they? That could have been one of us out in the snow — and no record of a breach in security according to your precious Marge!"

She was right, of course. I had taken to carrying a pistol, something I'd never done before — I no longer trusted my agency's ability to keep us safe. But that didn't have anything to do with whatever was happening in the lake. "Their equipment could still give us valuable data on the dimple."

"And how do we know whether we can even trust their data?"

I wasn't happy with how Marge had handled the security breach either, but I still thought Kelly was overreacting.

"What if I ask for the CAF Orion again?"

Kelly shook her head. "No. Not if they're sent by your NSA."

Damn me if I didn't let her talk me out of it.

She couldn't talk university research teams out of coming, though. Suddenly, interest in the dimple revived, and we were no longer as alone as we had been for years. It seemed like they were everywhere, bitching about agency controls on their equipment, about the mosquitoes, about how we wouldn't let them use the restrooms in the lodge. At least we still didn't allow the journalists clamoring for a permit into the park.

Kelly eyed the researchers suspiciously, as if they were going to take her dimple away from her or something. She sat in the tree fort and watched Emerald Lake with a simple pair of binoculars, jealous of anyone else who went near it. I joined her sometimes, but the more the lake changed, the more she left me. I didn't need that reminder of how far away she was again, not after we had seemed so close.

She was spending the day in the "dimple observatory" like usual when I brought her sandwiches one late autumn afternoon. We had the park to ourselves again for a change, for what little it was worth. The leaves of the maple around her were brilliant with shades of orange and red and yellow, but Kelly only had eyes for that damn dimple.

"Look at the way it's steaming," she said, hardly glancing at me as she took a peanut-butter-and-jelly. "Things are getting even warmer down there."

"Hm." I stared across the water, at the steam rising above the lake. It wasn't that hot, but there was enough temperature differential with the air to build miniature fog banks that rolled down inside the dimple and occasionally crept out. The first snow had not yet fallen, but the days were near freezing now. "You expecting anything?"

"Entropic progression is speeding up," she said instead of answering my question. "Coming up on the sixth anniversary of Nick's return."

Perhaps it *was* an answer.

※

By the time the snow started melting in late March, the dimple was so wide and shallow it spilled onto the shores of Emerald Lake, and it was developing a noticeable bulge in the middle. The water was quite warm.

The research teams had mostly disappeared over the winter. Alone again, Kelly and I had settled into a routine a lot like an old marriage — subdued acrimony, half-secrets, and mutual celibacy — so I was surprised when she came looking for me in my room in the lodge one day, with that huge smile I hadn't seen in probably a year.

I fell in love all over again.

"Bruce, can you help me with something?"

I tossed aside the tablet computer with the report I was writing. "Sure."

She led me down to the tree fort. In front of the trunk stood a big plastic shipping crate with rusted catches. I had never seen it before, although I recognized the chain saw and the plastic gas can next to it. There was fresh dirt clinging to the crate.

"What's this?"

"Something I buried a long time ago," Kelly said. "When I first got here."

Almost six years in the middle of nowhere together, and she starts pulling crates out of the ground? Entropic progression, my ass.

She was undoing the latches of the crate. "I need to get this up to the observatory. Do you think we can construct some kind of pulley system?"

"Okay. But what is it?"

"See for yourself," she said, throwing open the top. As I watched, she drew out a nice Celestron G-8 Schmidt-Cassegrain telescope.

※

"What are we waiting for?" It was cold as hell in the tree fort in the middle of the night, and Emerald Lake sounded like it was bubbling in the dark.

"April 8th, 2:30 am." Kelly trained the flashlight on her watch. "Which is in about twenty minutes."

I stared up at the stars. "He told you something in that phone call, didn't he?"

Her nod was little more than a shifting shadow. "There was more of a mission profile than we admitted."

I didn't miss the *we*. "You were part of it all along."

Kelly turned away from the Celestron, trained on Ophiuchus, low in the southern sky this time of year. "We had contingency plans."

Mission or no mission, she was finally showing me the core of her, the part she had kept hidden all these years. "So tell me."

She sighed, one hand trailing down the barrel of the telescope. "Obviously, we couldn't test his drive in advance. Nick was pretty sure he'd get a simultaneous translation to Barnard's Star, but he couldn't predict when he'd come out. One analysis said he'd just show up, the other that he had to wait out a lightspeed lag in a state of reduced entropy. Nothing's for free in nature, right? When he didn't come back right away, I knew he was waiting out the lag."

Assuming he hadn't just croaked out there in the depths of space in the violent spray of energy with which his home-built starship had departed. I shook my head. "How did he make the phone call from Barnard's Star?"

She laughed, her real laugh. And then I understood — the thing out there in the lake, the dimple, the masscon — that wasn't just a symbol of a man, someone I could compete with. No, that was her dream, the dream she shared with Nick MacInnes.

"The same paired-quantum effects that allow the drive to function can be used to open an electromagnetic channel," she lectured me. "We tested that here on earth. Once he got to Barnard's, Nick used a satellite phone with a virtual antenna that could hit the orbital network he'd built years earlier in our telecomm days. It totally blows Einsteinian simultaneity."

It dawned on me how ridiculous it was that a man went to the stars and called home on a cell phone. "You can say that again."

"It's how I knew we got the math right." In the dark, a ghost of a smile. "He didn't blow up when he got there. He called, promised to come home." Kelly leaned over, handing me what appeared to be a fat manila envelope. "Here."

"What is it?"

"Schematics, mission profile, the data about the cost-effective drive none of you believed in. Just in case things don't work out."

Things don't work out? What things? Her very slow entropic progression, presumably. I squeezed the envelope, checking the thickness of the paper, then slipped it inside my shirt. "Why me? Why now? I'm the enemy."

She put her face back against the eyepiece of the telescope. "Yeah, you are the enemy. You and all your government kind. But I also know you're an honorable guy. I've been hanging out here all these years to keep someone like you from messing things up. But you turned out okay, Bruce."

I swallowed. That was more than she had ever given me before.

She went on. "You're also a survivor. If it turns out we're wrong about something important, you'll get the data to the Canadian people for us."

I had questions, dozens, hundreds of questions about the documents in the envelope, but the warm, rotten reek from the lake bothered me too much to ask them. The Canadian Rockies in April are not supposed to smell like a Louisiana summer. After years of just sitting around, it was all coming together, too fast.

"Ophiuchus. You're looking for Barnard's Star. It's about six light years, right?"

"Five point nine seven," she said without moving her

head. She had her telescope where she wanted it and was staring intently. "Five years and three hundred and fifty-five days. Plus a few hours."

Emerald Lake was definitely bubbling now, like a pot on to boil. "Which is now, right?"

"Five minutes, give or take a slight margin of error."

"And you expect..."

Her smile gleamed at me briefly in the darkness before she turned her face back to the eyepiece. "A sign set in the heavens."

I suddenly remembered the bomb-pumped lasers. Below us, Emerald Lake was in full boil. Literally. The reeking steam was the mud bottom being cooked.

"Christ," I whispered. "You're watching for the laser light. He set off the Russian nukes, then hit his drive and came home."

"Got it. You Americans aren't all dumb after all. He'll be home a few seconds after we see the laser light."

I finally understood the slowly growing heat rise in the lake — it was energy leakage from whatever that masscon really was, some very exotic bloc of matter, a giant quark, something. Nick had been back for the last six years, wrapped in an indeterminate envelope of arrested entropy, sitting out reality in his lightspeed lag. Traveling through space and time, waiting for the equations to balance out and spit him out.

Kelly's husband was down in the bottom of the lake — literally waiting for his time to come.

The lake bottom. "He came out in hard vacuum, somewhere near Barnard's Star, right?"

"Yeah ... cometary orbit ..." She wasn't really listening.

"Why not come back to vacuum here?"

"Re-entry," she said absently. "Added an entire layer of complexity and design requirements. Throw weight for the launch, all kinds of issues. We figured on translating straight home."

Right smack in the middle of a much, much higher density of matter than the single hydrogen atom per cubic centimeter he would have encountered out in deep space. The burst of his arrival at Barnard's would have been nothing but a light show. Back here, though ... I was no physicist, but even I could imagine the energy gradient coming together when his wavefront finally collapsed out there in the lake.

"Kelly," I said, my voice as calm as I could make it. "Nick's ship is exploding. It's been exploding for six years, very, very, very slowly — that's what the dimple has been. In three minutes, it's going to explode in realtime."

"He didn't bring the nukes back." Kelly's voice was dreamy. "The ship was set to ditch them before re-engaging the drive. Just in case he couldn't set them off."

"Nukes or no nukes, something is blowing up. We have to go, *now*." I reviewed the escape routes, paths to higher ground versus how far we could get in my Ford Explorer parked up by the lodge.

"I said no nukes," Kelly replied absently, still peering through the Celestron.

"To hell with the nukes. He's carrying too much potential energy out there, without a hard vacuum to bleed it off into!"

Agonized, I could hear the smile in her voice. "The math worked. He got there, he'll get back. I have to be here to meet him."

She had a scientist's faith in the numbers, damn her —

and a lover's faith in the future. "For Christ's sake, no matter what the numbers tell you, Nick's ship is blowing up. Emerald Lake will be coming down around our heads." *Was there such a thing as a quantum explosion?*

"No. We modeled everything. We knew if he got there, he'd get back, and — Hey! Barnard's Star is getting brighter! I can see Nick's lasers!"

"Kelly, come on!" I broke my cardinal rule for dealing with her and tried to force the issue. Grabbing her arm, I pulled her away from the telescope, but she whirled on me. Her fist connected with my jaw.

"I'm not leaving, Bruce. You're afraid, *you* run."

And to my shame, I did. The instinct for survival won out, and I found myself scrambling down the ladder and running up the incline away from the lake and the disaster I was almost sure was about to occur. I decided against taking the extra time to find the Ford and get it started and just kept running uphill, for all the seconds left to me, leaving the woman I loved behind with her telescope and her dimple and her long-lost husband.

And then the lake exploded.

I groaned myself awake in a puddle of mud, wondering how long I had been lying there. What had once been Emerald Lake was awash with light, and I heard the chattering of a helicopter in the distance.

I had gotten far enough away. I was alive.

And Kelly almost certainly was not.

About a quarter mile away, I saw the remains of the lodge, splintered timbers rising above a sea of mud, a nightmare landscape of shadows and destruction glowing in a spotlight from above. With all that radioactive lake bottom blown everywhere, this place was a real hot zone now.

I pushed myself up, every joint screaming in protest. Coughing water out of my sinuses, or maybe blood, I turned to head back in the direction of the shore.

A pale glow in front of me turned out to be Marge, finding her way through the debris with a red-filtered flashlight. She was wearing street clothes — a knee length skirt, for the love of God, out here. "Glad to see you survived, Bruce."

And right behind her was Ray Vittori, the project manager from the Canadian Space Agency — who had told us about the radioactivity coming from the dimple in the first place.

And Vittori was in shirtsleeves, despite all the blown mud.

God damn, was I an idiot. So much for the radionuclides. No wonder my Geiger counters never worked right — they'd had to rig them up back at the agency. Hell, even *I* could think of three or four ways to fake a dosimeter.

"Nice to see you again, Agent Diedrich," Vittori said. "Although the circumstances could certainly be better."

I just stared at him.

He held out his hand, but it wasn't for a shake. It was palm up, expecting something. "I'll take those documents now."

"What — ?"

Marge smiled, teeth gleaming pink in the flashlit darkness as she lit a cigarette. "Microphones, Bruce. You should know better."

Yeah, I did know better. Passive surveillance was cheap. They could have wired the entire Canadian Rockies for sound during the time I'd been hanging around here.

I looked from Marge to Vittori. Kelly had said I should give the documents to the Canadian people, but I didn't think this was what she had in mind.

"There never was any radioactive fallout." My voice sounded as dead as I felt.

Vittori shook his head. "No."

"But why?"

He shrugged, finally lowering his expectant hand. "We already had all the data we were going to get from the dimple, Diedrich. All that was left was the woman."

The woman.

Kelly MacInnes, a laughing woman who had lived and died for a dream and a long-lost husband.

"Oh, God," I said, remembering someone else who was dead. "Sergeant Perry — ?"

Marge's expression hardened, and she took another drag on her cigarette. "Died in a hunting accident, Bruce. Headed the wrong way, you might say."

Hunting accident. Perry had found out something, been ready to say too much. I turned to her with the same question I'd asked Vittori: "Why?"

"There are plenty of people on both sides of the border who will do a lot for a working star drive."

For Nick MacInnes's plans, which we had all rejected twelve years ago. The Canadian who had made it almost all the way home from the stars.

With a sigh, I sat down on a shattered log, cruddy and mossy from the lake. Wedged behind it, I noticed a plastic gas container, the top still on.

"Can I bum a cigarette from you, Marge?"

"You quit years ago." Her voice was impatient.

"I need one now." I hugged myself, cold and wet in the dark April night. The envelope crinkled under my shirt, the one accurate record of MacInnes's cost-effective method of superluminal travel.

Marge held a lit cigarette out to me. I took it. "Thanks."

"Now smoke it and let's get going. There are some very important people waiting for you in Washington."

She turned to Vittori, whispering something I couldn't hear. Cigarette clenched between my lips, I twisted around and unscrewed the cap, pouring the liquid on the ground.

It didn't smell right — muddy lake water. The container

must have cracked from the force of the blast. I threw my cigarette into it. The butt fizzled and went out.

"You ready?" Marge asked.

I nodded. Pulling the envelope out of my shirt, I handed it over to the Canadian.

Some Canadian. I couldn't fool myself into thinking that it was what Kelly had wanted.

As we walked toward the helicopter, I realized I could no longer remember the sound of her laugh.

END

ABOUT THE AUTHORS

Jake Lake lived in Portland, Oregon until his death in 2014, shortly before his 50th birthday. His books include *Kalimpura* from Tor and *Love in the Time of Metal and Flesh* from Prime. His short fiction appeared regularly in literary and genre markets worldwide. Jay was a winner of the John W. Campbell Award for Best New Writer, and a multiple nominee for the Hugo and World Fantasy Awards. In 2015, he posthumously received the Locus Award for his collection *Last Plane to Heaven.*

Ruth Nestvold has published widely in science fiction and fantasy, her fiction appearing in such markets as *Asimov's, F&SF,* and Gardner Dozois's *Year's Best Science Fiction.* Her work has been nominated for the Nebula, Tiptree, and Sturgeon Awards. In 2007, the Italian translation of her novella "Looking Through Lace" won the "Premio Italia" award for best international work.

Blog: http://ruthnestvold.wordpress.com.

Other books by Ruth Nestvold

Looking Through Lace
Beyond the Waters of the World
The Future, Imperfect: Six Dystopian Short Stories
From Earth to Mars and Beyond

The Pendragon Chronicles:
Yseult: A Tale of Love in the Age of King Arthur
Shadow of Stone

Other books by Jay Lake

The Clockwork Earth Trilogy:
Mainspring
Escapement
Pinion

Green Universe:
Green
Endurance
Kalimpura

Printed in Great Britain
by Amazon